Dale Langlois

The Second Intelligent Species

The Cyclical Earth

Nick
thank you for
all the help
Dale Langlois
the Beaver

ISBN: 1-4810-5271-3
ISBN-13: 9781481052719

DEDICATION

This book is dedicated to my daughter, AJ and my son, Chris.
This book is not my legacy, my children are.

ACKNOWLEDGEMENTS

First and foremost I thank my father, Bruce Langlois who passed two years ago. He unknowingly gave me an artistic drive. He taught me how to make something out of nothing. I thank my Mother, Joan Jones, who always encouraged me when others thought I was wasting my time. I want to thank my daughter A.J. for teaching me to have the courage to be myself. My son Chris taught me anyone can do what others think you can't.

After this book was conceived, I needed the help of those with writing talents. The first person I approached was Doug Buchanan. A retired editor of a local newspaper, Doug gave me drive and hopes to follow a dream. He saw something in the story and pushed me on. Thank you, Doug.

Carol DeFord McClain and Tom Grady each hosted meetings in their homes. I loved being understood; we spoke the same language. Thank you, Carol and Tom and all who were there.

At Carol's first meeting, I met Linda Rondeau. A successful author, Linda not only taught me, but inspired me. Thank you Linda, you are my mentor.

I joined The Adirondack Center for Writing at Paul Smiths New York. There I met several famous authors, agents and publishers. I learned about the industry. Thank you Nathalie Costa Thill, administrator of ACW.

Thank you to my editor Meredith Efken at Fiction Fix-it Shop. A year and a half passed from the time she received my first submission till I was ready for the final line edit. Thank you, Meredith, for your patience.

The artist, who did my cover, gave far more than I paid for, and has become a friend. His encouragement and tips have been invaluable. Thank you, Dan Waltz.

I want to thank Lori Doughty Hickman. She came into the frozen Adirondack woods to take the photo on the back of this book. You are a true professional.

My slogan "Sci-Fi for the Working Guy" goes to all the people I work with at an aluminum smelter in upstate New York. I would love to thank all of them, but I know I would miss someone, and I am limited on space. One small group I must thank is my Alpha team (my Beta readers): Barry LaBar, Mark Goodfellow, Chuck Collins, Chris Adams,

Adam Crump, Pat Bronchetti, Nick White, Mike Gollinger, and my toughest critic Paul Fedoryk, Thank you. Without your input, this would have been a very different story.

Thank you to everyone at Alcoa, Massena West.

Finally to my loving wife Charlene, your tolerance is immeasurable. Thank you, sweetheart.

I hope you enjoy the read.

PROLOGUE

The world's population approached the twelve billion mark. Millions migrated. The problems of every landlocked nation changed almost overnight. The destruction of low-lying cities along the coasts of every continent pushed civilization inland, taking up valuable farmland. Global flooding destroyed another third of the planet's fertile soil. Farming moved north, but all too slowly. Famine plagued all nations.

A planetary power grid and bioreactors built to produce synthetic meat were the only solutions. They were astronomically expensive and took a big chunk out of every country's budget. When the true effects of mankind's carbon footprint became blatantly obvious to the taxpayers, the people who warned of the future problems of climate change were the first to be denied grant monies; funding for science seemed less important than money spent feeding the masses.

Concerns shifted to solving immediate problems and away from studying possible problems of the future. Telescopes lay idle all over the globe and in outer space. Fuel supplies and coolants ran out in existing space observatories; they were never replaced. Mars was unattainable. NASA no longer existed. Exploration was put on hold. Anything above the outer atmosphere was deemed unessential spending. Commercial spacecraft made regular flights to several In-Orbit Hotels where the affluent went to vacation in a zero gravity, Vegas-like atmosphere with planet Earth looming out every viewing portal. Space had gone commercial. The human race wanted to play in it before we learned more about it.

No funding was given for asteroid or comet observations, most of the objects considered a threat wouldn't hit until long into the future. The prevailing opinion was that there was plenty of time to develop ways to deflect a threat. Ninety-nine percent of all objects had been mapped and were being tracked.

"Some things come in hot," was the explanation given to the most powerful man on the planet. Nothing could be done. He and all the leaders of Earth unanimously agreed to keep the fate of their species a secret. It would be the last act of humanity.

Chapter 1
Good to Have a Choice

"Is that a real steak?" Beth asked. "I can see it now on the news, 'Local man, Nicolas Hunter was arrested for possession of non-certified beef. The offense will include a hefty fine, which in turn will result in one pissed off wife!'"

I knew she would bitch as soon as she saw them. Getting caught with unregistered, uninspected beef or any other animal tissue was a misdemeanor. All "Once Alive" meats must come from huge farms, strictly monitored by the federal government for safety and health, and the majority of that was reserved for the military. I think most of it gets eaten in Washington.

Everything else comes from the huge bioreactors popping up everywhere. Bioreactors are where Eco-Meats are cultivated, grown, harvested, processed and packaged. Raised in a vat from stem cells of living animal host, slabs of beef, pork and assorted types of fowl lay motionless at the bottom of a pool of steroid-rich brine. The two near Syracuse and the one in Watertown made three within two hundred miles.

"I work hard. I deserve the best once in a while. Yes, dear, these wonderful T-bones were walking two weeks ago. I'm sick of Phony Bologna. I need flavor, and I need texture. That test tube stuff tastes deader than dead. That's because it never lived. I need muscle, fat and gristle. I want to suck the marrow out of a bone. Tell me when you hear it sizzle on the grill if it is or isn't worth the risk. I'm sure the cops are eating steaks off the same cow right now."

"Who sold it to you? Did you buy it from someone at the farmer's market?"

"You know we don't reveal our sources. I didn't get it at the farmer's market. Nobody would try to peddle that stuff there. I was called out to relocate some raccoons, and the customer was so happy she gave me a couple steaks." My mouth watered like some Pavlovian dog. The petri dish stuff just can't give off that sound or that aroma of ...fat. "Come smell this."

"I'm just worried we'll get sick on it, it hasn't been inspected and who knows what the conditions were like where it was butchered. At least Phony Bologna is grown in a sanitary environment. This cow was walking in its own shit. I bet you got it from the Yoders. They're the only people permitted to have cattle."

"The Yoders are not the only Amish around, just the closest. Come on, Beth. You can't tell me you don't like the taste of real beef compared to that manufactured crap." I held the grill cover shut till she got close enough, and then rapidly lifted the cover to give her a smell. Smoke rolled under the cover catching Beth head-on.

Her head snapped back from the intensity of the heat. Once the smoke curled over her head, she wiped her eyes to focus on the two T-bones. "You better hope the breeze stays in this direction. You can certainly tell the difference. Nothing smells like real steaks on the grill."

"Will you stop worrying? Nobody's going to turn us in."

"No, I mean we don't have enough to share." She smiled and took another sniff. "Make mine well done, I don't want to get sick."

"You won't get sick; your stomach can digest far more than you think it can. You could eat this beef raw if you wanted to."

"Yeah, and I could eat bugs too, but you'll never see me munching on butterflies."

"Oh, that reminds me..." I ran to the truck and lifted the panel with the magnetic sign of my company, "Careful Critter Catchers," and took out the vacuum canister. I needed to incinerate all the cockroaches we'd collected this week. "Here, they're not butterflies, but I think they might taste the same."

"That's disgusting. You're going to catch something from the things you pick up someday. As long as it isn't rabies I guess I could fix you up. You don't incinerate them in here do you?" She lifted the grill top again to take another sniff.

"Hey, they won't cook if you keep lifting the lid."

She took one more sniff then closed the top. "Since when are you the expert on cooking steaks? How many have you grilled while we've been together?"

"I've barbequed more than you have, some while you were at work."

"That doesn't surprise me." She stomped off to the house shaking her head.

The only shaking I was interested in was the view as she walked up the hill to the house. Beth looked good in a pair of hiking shorts, even if they were a size or two too small. "Hey, get me a beer on your way out." Beth was my third wife. Building up a customer base and my devotion to the volunteer fire department in years past took more time than the first two wives wanted to give. I quit the service, but not the job. I made sure I spent more time with this wife. They say a smart man learns from his own mistakes; a wise man learns from the mistakes of others. I hope somebody has become wiser learning from my mistakes.

Beth returned seconds after I turned the steaks, handed me a beer, and opened one for her.

"Thank you. I'm going to go set a couple of skunk traps after dinner, want to tag along?"

"No, babe. I'm going to pick up the kids so they can spend the night." Although she was still a young sexy woman of forty-two, she had five grandbabies already.

"That's okay. I know you don't like Mrs. Spencer anyway."

Beth set her drink down. Beer foamed up and over the top, spilling off the picnic table to the ground. "You aren't going to help out that old bitch, are you? You know how much that family has messed up my life."

"I'm not doing it for her, I'm doing it for the skunks. I don't want them killed. I'll pick them up in the morning. Plus it's not that old lady's fault that you decided to quit teaching. That was your decision. We've been through this." I wiped up her mess.

"They didn't give me any other choice. I'm not going to teach anything I don't believe is the truth." Teaching science was Beth's passion, until she had a confrontation with a few parents about where humans came from one night at a PTA meeting. She refused to deny that Man evolved from apes and would not teach alternative theories, religious or any other. "If you catch any, make them piss on her front porch."

"Boy, you sure have a mean streak running through you. Must be the red hair."

"Kiss my ass, Nick." When Spencer's daughter told her kids that God killed the dinosaurs to make way for Man, and their teacher was just ignorant, Beth couldn't take any more. "Why try to teach the truth when the truth is being stifled? Since NASA fizzled out, nobody cares about science. At least with nursing, I can see results from my efforts." Her face took on the same color as her hair.

I decided to change the subject. "So how long are the kids staying?"

"They'll be staying the night," she snapped "but you'll have to watch them while I go to work tomorrow."

"Damn it, Beth, why would you invite them if you're not going to be here? What am I supposed to do; take them to work with me?"

"Yes, you can. You're your own boss. They'll love it. Let them play with the skunks, but so help me if I smell it on them, you will be giving them the tomato juice baths."

"Never mind. Mrs. Spencer will have to live with the smell a couple more days. I'm sure she's used to it." I could handle wild animals, but children pushed me past my own limits of bravery, and I wasn't about to have them tag along.

"Oh, one more thing, I lost the same diamond in my ring again, one of the little ones. Can you take it to the jewelers tomorrow?"

"This is the third time. I thought diamonds are forever?"

"They are, but the settings aren't. They're insured." The attention Beth gave her diamonds was rivaled only by her grandchildren.

I couldn't resist opening the grill cover; it had been almost three minutes. "Two more minutes." I rubbed my eyes and blindly said, "Get the other food together; I want to eat these while they're hot. Probably won't see a real steak again for a long time. I'm not going to want to go back to that other crap. I'm so sick of nugget this and breaded that. They're feeding us paste. It makes me sick to think of what I'm eating. I can only imagine some slab of flesh being extracted from a vat and placed on an assembly line of grinding and mulching machines, the excess fluids running off and used to nurture the new batch of stem cells for the next sixteen months until it's their turn to be harvested. The remaining mush would be breaded, baked, and bundled for mass sales: cheaper, eco-friendly, and easy to prepare. One minute in the microwave. Yum, just like Mom used to make."

The entrée: T-bone steaks marinated in Worcestershire sauce, accompanied by summer squash and portabella mushrooms swimming in margarine. Butter was deemed unsafe and unnecessary, (lovers of French cuisine disagreed). I also made some baked beans from scratch. We had more food than the two of us could eat, and all of it was real.

I clasped my hands and lowered my head to give thanks while Beth was up in the house searching for steak knives. Since we never needed them, I thought I would have time.

"Haven't we had this argument before?"

I guess she knew where they were better than I did.

"Do you really need to do that in front of me?" she said walking down the hill leading into the back yard.

I didn't mind missing grace when served Phony Bologna. It was made by man, and to tell the truth I wasn't all that grateful. "Dear, this meat had a soul. Something died so I can keep living." I never thought about that until they left no option but to eat the fake stuff. "I feel grateful and humbled to eat this cow and I wanted to thank somebody. You know how much I respect the animals I catch. I haven't euthanized an animal bigger than a rat in ten years."

"A: You should be thanking the Yoders, and B: the only reason you don't kill those stinking skunks, is when you pick one up at Mrs. Spencer's, you bring it to a woodlot near Mrs. Hampton's home where you can charge double to get rid of it."

"It's called job security, dear. I've even named two of them. I can carry Angel, the oldest one, to the truck without the cage, but the customer prefers I move it in a professional manner. At two hundred dollars a skunk, how can I argue?"

Chapter 2
Gluttony and Lust

Times were good and we wanted for nothing, except more time with each other and the kids.

After eating the banned banquet, I chased Beth into the camper, slapping her ass all the way up the rusting steps. For some reason the camper made her horny. That's where she hooked me, and that's where she always went when she was in the mood to be naughty. She was giving me all the signs. I could get lucky if I wanted to.

Paying more attention to her behind than to where I was going, I nearly knocked myself unconscious when my head hit the top of the door, (third time this year).

"You did it again, didn't you?" she said smugly, walking straight as an arrow, stretching her neck to hold her head held as high as she could. "Stubby people don't have that problem."

"We have to take advantage of every moment we have alone you know?" I held the top bunk until the stars ceased.

It was unbearably warm again this summer. Beth had been anticipating a vacation with the camper, but the season was near an end and work schedules seldom afforded us time together and probably wouldn't. Owning my own business meant never being far away just in case the church had another bat infestation. Neither the Pied Piper nor St. George were as welcome as the exterminator one hour before a wedding, and the new couple was willing to sign over their first born.

I put down the couch/bed to give us more room. Normally it killed my back, but I didn't expect to spend a long time in it. We weren't as limber as we used to be.

Beth closed all the shades, while I checked the fridge to see if there was any of my stash left from the party we had thrown last weekend. To my surprise there were two beers, the micro-brewery stuff, not our favorites, but cold. I opened up Beth's and handed it to her.

She plopped down onto the bed, nearly spilling it. "I really don't have time for this you know. I have to hang up clothes. The kids might pop in any minute." She always teased me into begging for it. She would lead me on, and then try to come up with an excuse why we couldn't play. "You know Sally wants me to help her on her science project." Sally is her granddaughter, named of course by her Ninny after Sally K. Ride, the first American woman in space.

Her hair caught my attention as it fell on her shoulders and across her breast. Lying on her side generated a cleavage bonanza. The freckles on her breast always enticed me. She loved tanning, even though she knew better. I bitched at her about it, but selfishly liked the way it made her chest look. She put a sticker of a couple of cherries on her left breast; it was the only area on her body that wasn't tanned. I couldn't take my eyes off the unforbidden fruit.

She tipped up the beer spilling some down her chin. I watched the beer trickle down her neck and into the vale of her cleavage.

"They had another Down's Syndrome baby born today down at the maternity ward: a little girl. The parents don't know yet, the results aren't in, and won't be till tomorrow, but I'm sure. She looks like Sally... She wants to build a volcano for the science fair you know?" Beth's favorite way to avoid sex is to start talking about her grandchildren.

It was my turn to come up with the excuse this time. My lust for her was overpowered by other forces. Thirty years ago, I would never have admitted I was too anything to avoid sex, but for now I was stuffed and couldn't if I wanted to.

"I wonder who put that idea into her head."

"She'll do the work; I'm just going to help her. Do we have any baking soda? We're going to build one that erupts and even spills out lava." Her past skills as a science teacher gave all her grandchildren an advantage over other kids in their class. They were all bright like their grandmother and didn't need the help, but Beth loved any chance to teach.

"Do you want another beer?" She left the camper and ran up to the house to check for baking soda and vinegar for the volcano. She came back carrying a hamper full of wet laundry. We needed to buy some vinegar.

"Where's my beer?"

"Oh, I'm sorry dear, I forgot it."

I wasn't surprised. "That's okay." I watched Beth hang the clothes. I couldn't take my eyes off her. The tan shorts clung to her cheeks. She stood on her tiptoes to reach the very top of the clothesline. Her red hair fell over her shoulders with all the natural curls that God gave her, though the color had been enhanced by man, or should I say the girl down at The Cut-n-Curl. Only when she dropped a sock or something and bent over, did the view improve. If I were a painter, there wouldn't be enough red to paint both her hair and the sunset, thanks to the girl at The Cut-n-Curl. "I'm ready to go back into the camper now," I said, as something caught my eye.

Something distracted me from drinking in Beth's splendor. I didn't know what it was I witnessed at the time. I thought I saw a flash of bright light towards the west. It didn't last long, and I wondered if I might have imagined it at first. Beth was still hanging up clothes. She didn't see it. I didn't mention it to her. I went back to watching her struggle with the laundry. She was too short on one end, and spent most of her time on her tiptoes—fun to watch. "The Orionids are visible tonight, how about we sleep outside and watch them?" Just as she said that, she dropped a clothespin.

"Naked?" The Orionids were some falling stars left by some comet or something like that. I didn't want to waste time watching the empty sky when I could be watching the ballgame.

"On second thought, I don't think so. There are too many mosquitoes. I'll get all bit up."

"I'll rub some salve on your bites." I walked up behind her and gave her the sign that the steak was no longer a problem.

I had been so infatuated with her, I forgot about what I thought I'd seen. My flirtations continued until a distant rumbling put an end to my psychological foreplay: a deep guttural reverberation from the bowels of the earth. It sounded like it was coming closer. I could sense it in my bones, and my heart. I just knew this wasn't going to be good.

Chapter 3
The Earthquake

Beth looked up at me and I down to her. The sound increased to a deafening thunder below our feet.

"Earthquake." Beth grabbed me by the arm.

I could see over the hedges into the next lot, where she couldn't. I saw the first ripple move the land. Then we felt it hit. The earth convulsed in a way I didn't think was possible. I would guess about a seven or eight magnitude earthquake hit our small town. I had no way of telling for sure its actual size.

Dust was emanating from the field adjacent to our property. The trees along the property line were shaking and losing their leaves. It was like Fall came and went all at once. The walls of our house flexed as the earth under it moved side to side. With each convulsion I expected the hundred-year-old two-story home to collapse.

I had lived there twenty-five years. We'd had an earthquake of about four point five on the Richter scale, eighteen or nineteen years ago. It rattled the windows and spilled my coffee. The water in the fish tank splashed around, and that was the extent of it. This one knocked Beth and me right off our feet. The earth was moving so violently that we slid along the ground enough to get grass stains on our clothes. We crawled up to the road to see down towards town. Power poles were snapping off. Sparks from the downed wires were dancing as the wires whipped. You could smell the electricity in the air. We could hear every window in town breaking, every car alarm was going off. Our attention was drawn to a loud cracking sound resonating from the back of our house. It was the sound of the back half breaking away from the main portion. Because the structure was built on a hill, when the smaller half broke away, it rolled down to the very spot Beth had been only moments ago. Thankfully, she had moved. The last time I saw the clothesline, it was being surrounded by a cloud of dust and what remained of the roof.

The tremors seemed endless. Besides the rumbling, car alarms, glass breaking, and dogs barking, the fire siren could be heard blowing a half-mile away. This rural town was the last to have one. They kept it for tradition only.

Breathing became difficult due to all the dust that had drifted from the collapse of our back addition. Insulation and dust drifted with the wind like the smoke of a campfire, always in the direction where you are standing.

After what seemed like a set of about three or four smaller earthquakes, all larger than the one I had experienced before when I was younger, everything just rumbled. I can't be sure how long we sat along the road looking and waiting for it to subside.

Beth was crying and shaking, and I was just kneeling, wondering what to do. I couldn't think from all the noise. I was experiencing sensory overload. What could I do? My house was broken in half, and the last remaining power wires in the country were lying on the car and truck. As I looked down the street I could see everyone else's home had taken as much damage as ours had, some maybe more.

We waited for the tremors to subside completely before we attempted to get to our feet. They decreased in magnitude, but the rumbling remained.

I felt Beth release my arm as feeling came back to my fingers. "Nick, there's not supposed to be earthquakes around here. Not this big. What to hell was that? Nick... the kids." She reached for her phone and struggled to push the same buttons she had pushed a hundred thousand times before without thinking. "I can't get a signal. I'll have to use the one in the house." Again we were the last people in New York to have a landline. "Sally should be home from school by now, shouldn't she?" She looked at her watch. She turned to run into the house.

"Wait a minute," I shouted. "Don't go in there until we check the place out. I don't think the rescue could get to us even if they wanted to. There are too many poles and lines in the road." The utility company was slowly eliminating them and replacing them with Tesla poles. T-poles delivered electricity to homes from a greater distance without the need of wires. Our town would need only five but I guess we were last on the list. People were slow to change in these areas. "This is going to take a long time to clean this up, maybe now they'll do away with them." I took her hand and led her up the steps. "C'mon, let's get your phone... go slow." I was looking for structural weaknesses in the walls.

The back half, where the kids' rooms are—correction, were—fell off and collapsed. Thank God they all moved out a year ago and it was just Beth and me. From the kitchen I could see right out into the back yard. Getting to the phone was not a simple task. Every dish and glass that we had in the cabinets was on the floor, directly in our path. The table and chairs were tipped over and shifted to the north end of the kitchen. The floor had sunk nearly three feet. The foundation near the back half had crumbled away.

I finally reached the handset and lifted it to my ear, "This phone's dead too, and all the power's out." I guess I could have told her that before we went into the house, but with all the confusion, I never thought about it. I was too busy watching the utility poles fall into the middle of the road. My mind had not put the two together.

In an outburst of desperation, Beth cried, "We can't do anything here. Let's go check on the kids. We've got to do something... Can we move the car or the truck?"

Both vehicles were unapproachable due to potentially hot wires. Just because there was no power in the house didn't guarantee there wasn't juice outside. I didn't want to take that chance. I had to come up with a plan to calm her down. "We can walk down to the fire house. They've got radios, and it's an emergency shelter. Plus they'll need every swinging dick they can get hold of." I guess I could have spared her from the "fireman talk." I had been a fireman for fourteen years in the same volunteer fire department. I guess it never really leaves your blood. My training kicked in. "Get all of our pills. We may be there a couple days. They'll have food and water. Plus they'll need the help. Get whatever else we'll need for two days. We'll be back by then; the insurance people will be next, then the carpenters. I've been meaning to remodel just one more time before I sell the place anyway."

I tried to reassure her but she was focused on the kids.

She threw some underwear, socks, our pills, and one change of clothes in her small travel bag. I threw some of my underwear, socks, deodorant, disposable razor, both our tooth brushes and toothpaste into a small backpack. "I am going to bring my kit with me." She had a trauma bag she carried everywhere.

"They will have all that down there. It's just one more thing we'll have to carry. We need to walk a half a mile to get to the fire station."

"I'm taking it and there's nothing you can do to stop me."

She grabbed her phone, and I grabbed my hat, backpack, and her bag, and we started to walk down to the station.

Chapter 4
The Fire Storm

Vigilantly we made our way around power lines. Some of them were still live and dancing along the ground, lighting the grass afire where they landed. Looking at them hurt our eyes, like looking at a welder's flash. I took Beth by the arm. She was so busy trying to get a signal on her phone that she narrowly avoided live wires. We walked up to Tom and Linda, my neighbors of fifteen years. I could see them standing outside surveying the perimeter of their home. Their property sustained severe damage. Their chimney had fallen and landed on their new hybrid SUV. It was one of the first vehicles to use the tesla poles as a source of energy, with a hydrogen backup. A big tree in their back yard had landed on their house, collapsing their roof down to the first story.

"Is everyone O.K.?" Beth asked. She walked over to Linda, who was crying and bleeding slightly from the bridge of her nose. Beth reached into her trauma bag and placed a folded bandage on her nose, tilted her head back, and said, "Don't worry, it looks a lot worse than it is. You might need to get glued back together, but I can't do that here. You don't want a scar do you?"

While Beth tended to our neighbor's nose, I turned to Tom and said, "Tom, we're heading to the fire department, why don't you and Linda follow us down?"

"We're going to church to set up the shelter there. I'm sure a lot of people will need a place to stay tonight. This town is going to need all the shelters it can get."

Something caught my peripheral vision. It appeared to be a dark thundercloud, but I'd never seen one like this before. It rolled with an orange glow to it, and it was moving fast. I noticed a grey fog coming from town. It was moving closer in rolling sheets. The closer it got the more I could tell it was smoke. I've never seen smoke do that before. Ribbons of smoke came down from the sky.

How could that be? I was confused. My past training told me that smoke goes up. I turned to find Beth.

"We've got to get out of here," she shrieked. She was looking past the smoke into town. She could see fires starting.

Linda screamed and ran into their garage that seemed to have escaped damage.

Beth dragged me towards a junk car that Tom was preparing for the demolition derby at the county fair.

Suddenly, I heard my neighbor Tom scream. I turned as we were running to see two ribbons of smoke rising over his back. He was swatting at his back as if hot bees had just stung him.

Then the Martin's dog got it too. I heard him yelp. He ran across the road with smoke trailing behind him, his tail tucked under his legs as he ran. That's when I noticed the BBs. There were thousands of burning BBs bouncing off the road like hail. Everything started to catch fire. I heard more screaming, though I'm not sure who it was.

Beth's yanking me into the car woke me up. I was in a state of utter disbelief. "What to hell is going on?" Beth asked as she slammed the door on my leg.

I pulled it away to let her shut it fully. I couldn't answer. I felt burning on my neck. I swatted at it as if a bug were there, but this was fire. The burning remained as the embers melted into my shirt and could not be shaken free.

"I have no idea, but if we stay here we're going to die." The leaves that were caught in the old car's windshield started to burn.

Beth screamed and grabbed me. "Don't let me burn alive. Nick!"

I turned in my seat to see what she screamed at. I looked out the window and saw Tom on fire, running into his house. The shrubbery on the side of the road was ablaze.

We saw a car slide off the road in an attempt to dodge wires, the tires screeching as it slammed into one of the last remaining utility poles. The occupants were able to get out of their vehicle, but as soon as they stepped out, they jumped right back into their burning car.

There was smoke coming into the car that we were in. Its paint was starting to burn, and the air was getting very warm and smoky inside.

"Nick, do something, hurry, I'm scared, Nick please." Beth was so afraid, and so was I. I didn't have a plan and thought we would both die in that car. We coughed to the point that unconsciousness could soon follow.

I looked out the window through all the smoke and I saw a place where there was none. Down near the water leading into the culvert under the road, there wasn't smoke, but steam. There was water in that ditch.

I opened the door and yelled, "C'mon." I stepped out into a rain of fire. I had Beth's arm and was pulling her out. That's when she pulled back and slipped free.

The embers had already started to get down my neck and the back of my pants where my plumbers crack is. They burned like hell. I wasn't in the mood to argue at the time. I reached in the car, grabbed a handful of her red hair, and pulled her to the door.

I yelled in the loudest most convincing voice I had. "Look, it's wet and cool in there. It's our only chance. C'mon!" My neck and back were burning. I just wanted to get to the water. The little BBs of molten material were burning my wrist too, as they got in under my watchband. I took it off and threw it, along with my backpack. My hair not under my hat was smoldering. I grabbed Beth's arm and gave it a yank, she slid out of the car to her feet in one fluid motion. We both ran screaming towards the culvert. Even the pockets of my jeans were catching those little BBs. You couldn't escape them. I looked back at Beth, and her beautiful red hair was ablaze. I reached out and threw her towards the culvert. We both hit the water at the same time. We skipped along the surface like two stones thrown by a child. We rolled around splashing water on each other.

This put the fires out, but the air was chokingly hot. Our breaths were taken inches from the water. Beth scrambled up into the culvert. My nose was right up her ass, pushing her into the tube even further. She was screaming and kicking all the way, but my ass was the last thing that was out in the fire, so naturally I insisted. I splashed water on my neck, she splashed it on her head and everywhere else where we burned, my pockets, my neck, down the crack of my ass, in her cleavage. We burned all over. We inched up into the culvert, only about three feet in diameter, and then we reached a T in the tunnel. I just followed Beth. She led us to the good air, and deeper water. That's what saved us. We were in an area with enough oxygen to live, and the water kept our bodies cool.

Beth stayed in the water as I snaked back out to the opening to see what was going on. I couldn't get all the way to the end due to the great heat, though the sounds told the story. Every house in the neighborhood was on fire at the same time. The unmistakable sound of a structure collapsing is familiar to any fireman who's heard it once. I could hear explosions in the distance. The heat and smoke forced me back into the culvert. There we stayed for what seemed an eternity.

The air almost abandoned us. We had to keep our mouths near joints in the culvert, where fresh air seeped in. I thought I was going to pass out a couple of times. The air was so hot it felt like our lungs would quit working. Whenever I could talk, I checked to see if Beth was still alive and coaxed her to keep trying and not to give up. We almost suffocated several times.

I have no idea how long we lay in that culvert. Sooty water washed over us all day and all night, though we could only estimate when that was.

We could see the glow of the fires on the cement wall for about a day, and then it got dark. We didn't dare move. The air was so superheated that we barely lifted our heads out of the water, only to breathe at that seam in the tile. That's where the best air was. I know we shouldn't have, but we drank a lot of water in that culvert. It was so hot; it felt like we were sweating underwater.

I found myself falling asleep with water running alongside my face, but somehow kept it above water. Instinct forced my head above water so I could stay alive. The same thing happened to Beth. We lived through the most horrible scenario never imagined by man, and I think most of it was because of instinct. We stayed in that culvert and neither one of us said a word to the other one. We just lay there sucking up the fresh air when it was given. We both went into a dormant stage, a survival mode. Our main purpose in life was to survive. At that time, that meant breathing. We talked when we thought things were starting to get better, when we could breathe freely, without hacking.

The odor of the air was putrid: a sickly sweet, acidic smell of burning wood, plastic, grass, rubber, and hair. We had nothing else to do but lie there and pick apart the smells in that culvert. I even think I smelled popcorn once. When you've been a fireman, the smell of burned hair never leaves you. Both of us had burned hair and when it gets wet, it smells three times as bad.

Every now and then a rat or muskrat would swim up along our backs, over our shoulders, and on up into the rest of the culvert. Beth freaked out the first couple of times, but then discovered that the less she moved, the quicker they left.

It started raining and the water inside rose quickly. It didn't take long to get to a dangerous level. I was glad to hear her scream when the waters rose, a sure sign she was still alive.

"Get out, get out!" I screamed to her over and over again. We could barely breathe the air, but I knew we couldn't breathe the water.

We both washed out on the same side we came in, out of a pitch-black culvert into the pitch black. Slowly, we glimpsed fires still burning, even though it was raining. These were people's houses, or what was left of them.

We crawled up out of the slime and the muck, up onto dry land, only to see Tom's house burned to the ground. I looked east, and by the glow I could see my house about two stories lower than it had been before we went into that tunnel. Funny, I knew that's what I'd see, but I never thought I'd see it.

Chapter 5
Heroes and Truth

The air was acidic and thick with odors—a nauseating olfactory gumbo that caused our lungs to burn. We climbed out of the ditch, and as if on cue, dropped to our knees and started to vomit and cough uncontrollably.

After we caught our breath and stood up, we started down the road. No houses remained. The only light came from pits of burning rubble. All the trees we could see were smoldering, just the bigger limbs remained.

"Nick, was that a nuclear bomb? This is a living nightmare." She could hardly speak. After spending that long in the culvert, I thought she was doing tremendously.

I just kept quiet trying to make sense of it all. *Why would terrorists set off a nuclear bomb in this area? There's a sparse population, no political, industrial or military targets around here. What else could have done that to everyone? Why would a bomb start with an earthquake?*

We continued to walk towards our house. It didn't take long to see it was gone. All that remained above level ground were the metal shells of our vehicles and the grandkids' swing set.

"Nick ... the kids... Oh my Go—" She stopped herself.

"Come on. Let's go find them." I took her by the hand. We turned back towards the fire station. We had to get some help and the only place I knew to get it was at the station. Plus I knew they would have some answers about what hit us. They had radios and would be in touch with anybody and everybody. I also remembered they had some "weapons of mass destruction" training.

The heat was stifling. The rain had stopped and the fires began to intensify. Radiant heat came from every cellar we passed, and it felt like being in an oven. Our clothes were wet and steam would roll off us if we stood too long near one of our neighbors' houses looking to see if anyone survived. We dried out fast but we got some steam burns. We had to keep running in and looking, then running away to the darkness to cool off. Nobody was left alive. How could they be? How many people had found a culvert full of water fifteen feet away from them when it started getting hot?

The odor of burnt flesh wafted from each car we passed, and could be smelled as far as thirty yards away. The people looked like mummies frozen in black charcoal, mouths wide open begging for mercy. Maybe they had received more mercy than Beth and I.

By the time we approached the four corners of town, we had yet to find one home still standing, or one abandoned vehicle. Nobody had tried to get out.

We made it to the fire station. It didn't take me long to figure out what happened here. The trucks were all out on the pad. Hose covered the ground, still connected to the engine. We walked past burned bodies on the ground. My friends were lying around, under, or in the trucks. Their personal protective equipment was no match for the intense heat they'd experienced. The Nomex protective bunkers and jackets still retained their original shapes, though crusty and discolored. Each detail of stitching was recognizable, though the member in the gear wasn't. Except for the rookies, each wearer's name was monogrammed on the front and back. These were all neighbors and friends that I used to spend time with. In a sense, Beth saved my life; if I hadn't met her, I would have been down here with them.

After Beth saw all the death and destruction, she realized that her kids could never have made it. It was just a freak thing that we had. We were in the right place at the wrong time. No matter how you put it, the odds of anyone else being alive in this area were extremely low, but we still had to check.

We decided to walk the road and go two towns over where her kids lived. There was another fire station there. Maybe that area had been spared. Maybe her kids made it to safety.

I kept thinking that the sun should be coming up any time now. We spent a majority of the time walking in the dark, feeling for the side of the road with our feet. The trip, which normally took ten minutes in the car, stretched on for what felt like five or six hours. When we got near her kid's house, we looked for a glow in the distance like we had seen at other houses. None could be seen.

"Does that mean that they might have made it? Maybe their place was spared." She was looking for any chance at hope.

We arrived at the dip in the road near the kid's house. "Sit here until I get back." I hated to leave her.

I'd never seen her helpless. Her face was blank and emotionless. She sat down on the roadside bank. There wasn't much else left to sit on.

As I walked away, I kept looking back to make sure she wasn't following. I could scarcely make her out against the glow of the last house we passed. Only the cellars had light in them now. There's a lot of fuel in a house and it all settles in the cellar. It burns and smolders for days, sometimes weeks. That's why we couldn't see her son's house glowing in the distance. His house was a one-story house built on a pad with no cellar. All the fuel lay on the ground, bombarded by the hot BBs. There was nothing left to smolder or burn. I wasted little time looking. Nobody could have survived that.

I tried to run to the nearest culvert in the road, but with all the smoke, running was impossible. Out of breath, I got down on my knees and looked in. "Kids?" I asked, with little expectation of a response. "Kids?" I repeated, quiet enough that she couldn't hear.

I turned around and headed back to where I'd left her. I could see her, still looking off into the darkness. Her silhouette was that of a woman who already knew the answers.

"Let's head to their fire station. They could be there." I took her hand, and when she got up I put her on my left side. We walked by her son's house. She never looked to her right. We just kept walking, and neither one of us said a word. We walked in the dark towards the next town. Every home, farm, and business was gone, burned to the ground.

The next town was about a mile ahead. I realized that neither one of us had eaten in two or three days. I'd lost my appetite.

I couldn't decide whether to keep trying or not. What was the sense of it? Could it be possible that we were the only survivors? I kept checking culverts along the road. If we thought of taking refuge in one, somebody else might have.

I wondered how far we needed to go to get out of the blast zone. It had to be better just around the next bend. Why was it still so dark, and why the earthquake? I was still thinking of a bomb.

We eventually arrived at the next town, which was just as desolate and leveled as the others. It was difficult to know exactly where we were. The only point of reference was the train rails coming into town.

When we got to the fire station, we found the same scene as our town. They also had fought to the bitter end. There must be a gene in firemen that makes their will to live to be so strong. Their station was also burned to the ground, but their training building wasn't. It was built entirely out of concrete. Talk about pure irony. The only building left standing was one built to catch fire every time it was used.

Chapter 6
The Basics of Survival

I pushed the metal door open with my foot since it was still too hot to grab with my bare hand. It swung open, but it was so dark we couldn't see. Beth stood holding the door open with her foot.

"I'll be right back, don't move." I ventured off into the darkness.

"Don't you leave my here alone. Get back here, Nick. Nick? God damn it, Nick." She knew I'd be back.

After returning from gathering wood, I ventured into the burn shack. Two firemen had taken cover inside. They'd escaped the flames, but not the heat. Their bodies needed to be moved to the back away from where Beth and I would be spending the night. The first attempt to move one resulted in flesh being torn from the arm of the first man. Dragging them by their bunkers, I cleared an area for us to start a fire and rest.

Beth sat and cried while I worked.

It didn't take me long to build a small fire using coals from the back room of the training building. This was the same fire that wiped out everything we knew in our world. All of the people we loved died a horrible death. Her children died in agony, while we lay in a culvert like a couple of rats.

This fire was as necessary to us as the air we sucked up along the inside of that culvert. Now we were in control of it again. It lit the walls and we could see what we were up against. We looked clearly into each other's eyes for the first time in days. Soot ran down her face like a glamour girl's mascara in the rain. I held her until we needed more wood, neither one of us said a word.

I gathered up more wood. It wasn't too hard to find, I just looked around the edge of cellars. There was always some that didn't burn all the way. I brought Beth a lot of wood so she would feel comfortable. We needed it for the light and not the heat. It was plenty hot enough.

We needed to get water and fast. With this elevated heat we wouldn't travel much further unless we got some water, and food. I had to sit and think about it. I had to think about it for a long time. All the Seven Elevens were out of business. The rivers and streams were so full of soot and ashes, the water had to be bad. The rain had stopped, and when it had been raining, I hadn't thought of catching it. I had been hoping that help would be around the next corner.

"I think we have to help ourselves from now on. Stay here. I'm going to look for a pizza place. You want anchovies?" I wasn't sure if the timing was right for comedy, but I had to try to get some life back into her eyes.

"How long are you going to be gone?" She was still pissed at me for leaving her alone at the door earlier.

"Not too long. I'm going to see if I can find something at the supermarket, try to find some water, or a cold beer." I tried one more time at the comedy thing. Getting the same response, I turned to go into town. "Be right back."

"Get me one too," she said with barely enough enthusiasm to get the words out.

I'd take it. She retained some of her sense of humor, although it was buried beneath layers of other emotions.

I walked to where I thought the corner store was, and carefully stepped into the debris. No door was necessary. I immediately stepped on a nail, through my sneaker, and into the thick part of my foot, luckily not too far into the skin.

I needed to see. I searched for more wood to use for a torch, and quickly found enough, along with the fire to start it. It wasn't the brightest, and I had a hard time keeping it going. I found that by holding three boards together, the fire would last longer. I walked back to the store and carefully picked my way around the debris and the dead bodies. People had run into the store when the firestorm came, but it was no escape. The remains no longer resembled bodies, more like bones surrounding a pile of guts that smoldered and emitted the stench of death. I'd been getting so used to death, these were just more obstacles to step over.

It took a while to find a couple of good cans lying in the rubble, a few were protected from the majority of the heat. Labels were burned off, but they looked fine other than that. Any other cans I found were opened by the heat or crushed when the roof collapsed.

I tiptoed to where I thought the front of the store was, and rummaged around for a while. The glass to the display case lay shattered on the floor. Looking through the ashes and coals, careful not to get too close to the hot ones, I noticed a familiar shape.

"That's a knife," I said aloud, as if there were somebody listening. I reached down and picked it up, then just as quickly dropped it. It was still quite hot. I picked it up again and blew on it as if it were a piece of hot corn on the cob. I put it in my pocket once I was sure it was cool enough. It went straight to the ground. Both pockets had the bottoms burned out. I should have known. I was suffering with blisters there on both legs.

The knife had a hole for a strap. I needed to devise a way to hook it to my jean's belt loop. Copper wire lay all around, power no longer flowed through it. My new knife was assigned its first job: cutting wire. I was careful to use the part near the handle. That way, the rest of the knife would stay sharp. A valuable find. The blade was in good shape and it still locked in place.

I fashioned a makeshift strap out of copper wire. I carried three cans of food and a new knife. Water still escaped me. I would have to think about that one a while longer.

I made my way back to the training building, or "smokehouse," to find Beth with a faraway look of hopelessness, staring at the fire and its reflection flickering on the wall.

I tried to walk in without frightening her, but as soon as I spoke, her body convulsed like she had received an electric shock.

"Damn it. You could've let me know you're back."

"I found some food...sorry didn't mean to scare you. Found three cans. Don't know what they are. I found a knife too...see?"

"Did you find a can opener, Einstein?" Her sarcasm was the first sign that she had some of the old Beth left in her, thank God.

"Yes, I told you I found a knife. It's not a Swiss army knife but it will work."

"It smells different in here," she said, but I wasn't paying attention. I was too busy trying to open one of the cans. I was starving now and really wanted to know what was in this can.

"What did you say?" I said, concentrating on opening the can, careful not to cut myself.

"It smells different in here. Outside you smell burned rubber, plastic, and death. In here the only smell is burned wood or hay. If I have to choose between the two, I pick in here." She didn't know about the two men I pulled to the back of the building out of her sight.

I pried with the knife to open the first can. "It's corn." I reached out my arm and handed the can to Beth. "Here, drink the juice too. It may be the only source of water we'll get for a while. It smells okay and it's still warm. Be careful not to cut yourself on the jagged top."

She smelled her corn.

"You eat that one, and I'll take the next one." I started to open the second can. I'd already learned to put the can on the floor and open it from the top by kneeling directly over the can, pushing the blade straight down. Once it started to cut, I pushed down on the back hard, then rotated the can and repeated the process until I got back to where I'd started. Not pretty, but it got the food out. Funny to think I had been so careful not to ruin the blade when I was cutting the wire. Now look how I abused it.

"You take half of this. Maybe those other ones are spoiled," Beth said.

I had already finished opening the second can. "That's okay. I've got this one open already. This one's corn too. I'll eat this one, and you can eat the last one."

I tipped the can back, and it tasted like corn that could have been served to the Queen. "I hope the next one is T-bone steak in a can." My guess was corn.

Three tries into this, and I could open a can in about one minute. "Save these cans. We need to collect some water." We both had diarrhea from the water we drank in the culvert, and I knew we were dehydrated.

"Why bother, Nick? What's left to live for? The kids are all dead. Everyone's dead. Everything is gone. Burned. It's all gone, Nick. We've been blown back to the Stone Age. I think I'd rather be dead than try to live in a world like this."

The only thing I couldn't accept was to hear her give up, because without her I wouldn't have a reason to go on. "No!" I had to put a stop to this right now. "Shut up right now. God damn it. We spent how long in that fucking tunnel? How far have we come to this spot? The kids are gone, everyone's gone. That's right, there's nothing anybody can do about it. Didn't you see those firemen? Those bastards fought for the last breath they got, in both towns. They were torn between saving their own lives and saving the lives of other people running up to them on fire. They were pumping water out of trucks that were fully involved in flame. They had too many victims to save. This ex-fireman only had one life to save, and I did that, in that tunnel, and I'm going to keep doing it no matter what you say. There's got to be someplace that wasn't hit as bad. We're going there tomorrow, we're going somewhere tomorrow." I drank the last of my corn juice to cool my temper. It wasn't enough to quench my thirst, but would keep me going until I got some sleep. We were both exhausted. We needed rest.

"Now please eat your friggin' corn. I love you so much." I offered her share of the last can to her.

She silently looked up at me... then down into her can of corn.

Chapter 7
Scavenging

I awoke to a shower of sparks and Beth's scream as she ran out the door into the dark.

"Why didn't you tell me there were two dead guys in there? Why didn't you drag them out?" She threw the burning board she was using for light right at me, just missing my head. More sparks fell to the ground.

"I didn't want to scare you last night." I picked up the stick of wood and blew on the embers till a flame rekindled.

"I'm not spending another night in there!"

"Alright, we're going to head for Syracuse."

"That's over two day's walk, Nick."

"Do you want to stay here?"

Her lack of response was her answer. "Wait here and I'll make up a torch or two." I went back inside to see what could be found for material. The two firemen's street clothes had not suffered any fire damage. Stripping them took more stomach than I could manage for long. I took off the T-shirt of each and went back out with Beth. Disturbing the bodies released an odor I could no longer deal with, but the two shovels inside were going to be our handles once the bottom was broken off. The smell was tolerated until the job was finished. The fire trucks still had baked-on grease around the undercarriage. I scraped off enough to take with us.

Beth held up some burning wood for light. "Nick...what do you think happened?"

Setting the cloth downwind, I answered, "I thought it was a bomb at first, but now, I don't know." I couldn't think and work at the same time.

"You know what I think it was, or do you? You never listened to me when I talked about science before. You probably don't want to hear what I think happened. You listened to your minister talk about God more than you listened to the things I talked about."

"That's not true, dear. I can't help but hear the things you preach to me. You are very persistent."

"I think it was some kind of impact, like the one that wiped out the dinosaurs."

"Come on, Beth. Everything in space has been found and they've been tracking stuff like that for years." Spreading the crusted grease on the cloth, I went back to work.

"Only amateurs are looking. All the big telescopes are shut down. Even though the space junk and asteroids we know about are being watched, a comet could have snuck through, but I think an amateur astronomer would have found it. Someone must have noticed it. Why wasn't there a warning?"

"Could it have been something from the sun?"

"I thought maybe because of the fire, but that doesn't explain the earthquake." She blew on the makeshift torch to increase the light. "It could be the result of something mankind has never experienced."

I set the finished torch down. "What do you mean by something we haven't experienced?"

"I've told all of this to you before. This proves you've never listened to me."

"I'm listening now!" I said.

"There are things in space that could affect us here on earth, even though they're many light years away. It could have been a gamma ray burst, but again the earthquake doesn't make sense. A supernova of a star closer could have accounted for both I guess, but I think we would continue to get hammered by shock waves." She looked down and all my attention was on the second torch. "You're not listening again! I don't know why I bother."

"I'm sorry, hon. I was caught up with this."

She slammed her fist down on her leg. "What gets me is that they might have seen it coming. Those bastards are probably hunkered down in some bunker somewhere. We've been left to fend for ourselves. There was no warning whatsoever. This is a mass extinction event. They had to have known it was coming."

"Now you're getting stupid. I agree the impact thing, or the solar flare thing or whatever, could have happened." The embers from the proto-torch ignited the newer improved version. "But we're not extinct, and we're not going to be. We are a lot smarter than the dinosaurs. See, could a dinosaur do this?" The light from the newer model outshined the old one, tenfold.

"Nick, do you know there have been at least five mass extinctions in the past? It's all in the fossil records."

I knelt there in silence thinking. The only sound was the wind blowing the flame on our new torch. That's when I realized the magnitude of our situation. I just looked off into the darkness, until some hot grease splattered onto my wrist to bring me out of it. "We're going to find more people, we can't be the only ones left alive. We need to get a whole bunch of food and supplies. We need to find clean water. We need to do this now. C'mon let's go back to that store."

I helped Beth get up and led her by the hand, out of the last structure we might see standing for miles.

The store I had visited the night before was still open, so we just walked in. The floor was difficult to find because the roof had collapsed, and the steel took on twisted shapes that no longer contained right angles. Beneath the steel were hot coals, so we didn't look there. There were areas where the rain stopped the fire before it could ruin everything. Cans of food that survived were found in those places.

I pawed around in the rubble for cans, then tossed them to Beth who was standing outside the building's perimeter, ever alert for boards containing nails. She would pile them to avoid stepping on one. She also stacked the cans until we could find something to carry them in.

"Look for a can opener... and pots or pans. Cast iron cookware doesn't burn."

I was going to say something smart-assed, but I held my tongue. I was glad to hear her speaking and thinking about how we were going to get through this.

We had about fourteen cans up to the point that I found the mother lode. What used to be a case of crushed tomatoes lay at my feet. The crate had burned away, but some labels remained.

A can opener still escaped us, but I did find some magazines that weren't totally destroyed, the edges were burned off, but the middle was still readable. I threw them to Beth. "Here you can read these when you get bored."

She piled the magazines, just like she did the cans and pieces of wood she'd gather, while I was looking for a can opener. Then I realized that we were looking in the wrong place.

"Hey, we're not going to find a can opener here, we need to look in people's houses, where their kitchens were. That's where you'll find your pots and pans too." Suddenly I sensed guilt about rummaging around in the burned down homes of dead people. Just as quickly, I realized once again what we were up against. "There's one across the road."

"I'm not stealing anything from..." Then common sense hit her too.

Morals didn't matter right now. Nobody was left to judge us. We only had to answer to ourselves, and my God.

Chapter 8
Another Survivor

Our stash consisted of one hundred forty-two cans of food, and a walk-in cooler of canned drinks. Some bottles had even made it—a lot of it was beer. We had hit the jackpot.

There was no way we could carry all of it with us, and there was no reason to stay in this town. Nobody had survived here. We had to move and try to find other people. There was strength in numbers. Maybe we could find some area that didn't get hit so badly.

We took a break and opened up a few cans of food. Beth insisted that we eat a can of tomatoes; they were full of vitamin C. We filled up on soda and beer, even though Beth said that I shouldn't drink only beer. I assumed that these would be the last I would see for a long time.

We had to find something to carry as much as we could haul. "We need to find a wheel barrel." I said as I tipped back my third beer.

"Stay right here and rest, I'll be right back" She grabbed her torch, lit it off mine and headed into the darkness.

"Hey, you be careful," I said. Taking her advice, I opened another can. *Hmm, pork and beans.* I quickly wolfed them down before she came back. It felt good to have a full stomach, even though this was canned food. I seldom bought it when we shopped, though Phony Bologna wasn't any better.

Beth must have found something because I heard the loudest racket. She was coming down the road with not one, but two kid's wagons: the metal ones with the rubber tires. The only problem was, some of the rubber on the wheels hadn't burned off completely. It sounded like a whole herd of those shopping carts that I always got, those that had a tire squared off on one side. I think she was just dragging one. Because the wheels wouldn't move it was sliding sideways.

"This ought to carry what we need." She was so proud that she had done her part. "All I had to do is look for a backyard that had a swing set." She was in this as long as I was. It made it so much easier not to go through this alone.

I stood up to see her new find. "Great. Bring them over here, and I'll fix those tires." These would be a great asset. I didn't think we needed all the cans, but we could carry most of them. We continued eating the canned food and drinking warm beer and soda. Beth found a can of peaches, and she shared them with me. I gave her one of my beers. I felt guilty about the pork and beans.

When we finished eating I cleaned all the rubber off the metal wheels of the wagon. They still didn't roll quietly, but they did roll straighter.

We loaded as many cans of food into one wagon as it would hold. The other was filled with soda and beer. Beth took the magazines. The remaining cans of food, drinks, and piles of wood were left near the store in case other survivors stumbled into town.

We had to learn to adapt. We made the best of what was left. It wasn't easy pickings. Most houses had cellars, the climb down was too dangerous, so we did all our picking in houses that didn't have cellars or in garages of those that did. The garage was the only place that wasn't eight feet lower than ground level.

In the first house we searched, we found a can opener to the right of the range. Five minutes or so of digging turned up forks and knifes and spoons. We each kept one fork and one spoon, I already had a knife.

A small ax was added to the wagons. The hatchet once had a wooden handle surrounding a metal shaft, but of course the wood had burned off. Duct tape took care of that problem. We found a roll in a fridge some guy had used as a storage cabinet in what was his garage. This stuff was one of the greatest inventions man ever made. I just wrapped the handle a half dozen times with duct tape and, voila. We made a makeshift back-pack out of a burned one we found. We used the remaining duct tape to weave a sticky basket around the frame. I even found some fish line and fishhooks in a tackle box that had melted around most of the lures.

We knew our whereabouts because of the road signs, even though the paint had burned off. The stickers that reflected light had melted, but still could be read. "We've got thirty-six miles to go before we hit the city," I said. "I know we'll find people there. The odds have to be better just because of the sheer numbers. There are tunnels, and every building has three or four floors under the ground. There were sprinkler systems, and so many more places to hide and take cover." I stopped talking to hack up a big chunk of lung butter and then spit it out. All the smoke I'd been breathing really messed up my lungs, even more than when I was in the fire department. Maybe I was just getting cleaned out. I was even hearing Beth bringing up crap. I hadn't heard that since she quit smoking dope. It was at that point another cough was heard, and it wasn't Beth.

Running towards the sound brought us to a figure sitting up against the remains of a vehicle. He coughed again. As the light from our torch reached him one thing drew my attention. A patch of white around his neck stood out in contrast to his burnt flesh. In all my years as a fireman, I had never seen anyone survive such burns and survive. Somehow this priest was still alive.

"In Jesus' name it shall be done." He attempted to make the sign of the cross. His whole arm trembled, stiff and weak. His hands were swollen and skin hung down from his face. No hair remained, and his eyes were slightly opened, oozing with fluid. It was impossible to distinguish clothing from skin. They had melted into one, except for the collar, which looked untouched.

Beth grabbed a soda from the wagon and knelt down. "Here drink this." She opened it and lifted the drink to his lips.

With a burst of energy he raised his hand, knocking the can to the ground. "You have been sent to me by Christ."

I picked up the can before it all spilled out. "Here Father, you need to drink." Again he refused.

"No it is you who need to be saved. I have been chosen to stay behind to save one more. You are the one." He strained to look up at Beth.

All the doors of the car he was next to were open. "Father, were you with anybody else?"

He slowly pointed to the guardrails without lifting his arm. "There," he said.

"They might have survived." I slid down the embankment, more on my ass than my feet.

I looked into the dark void for a place where passengers could have survived. *Nobody.*

Then I found them. A father and his two daughters lay motionless in the water, the girls beneath him. Their hair was long and blond, best I could tell. He took all the fire to protect his babies. His shoulder blades and backbone were showing as a result of all the heat. The back of his skull shined in the light of my torch. His daughters died of drowning while he tried to keep them from the inescapable heat. I can only imagine the conflict in his mind during the end of his life. Keep his daughters under water away from the intolerable heat, or let them up in an attempt to breathe the burning air that surely would have killed them immediately.

I'm glad Beth had stayed up on the road with her patient. I've never told her of what I found. If there's such a thing as power-weeping, that's what I did. She didn't have to know. Even though a nurse, she never witnessed the things we'd seen these last few days. She didn't need to see any more.

Chapter 9
The Gift

I composed myself and made my way up to Beth. She knelt next to the only person we'd found alive. Her hands were in a position I'd never seen her take. Was she praying? I couldn't believe my eyes. "How's he doing?" I asked.

Her arms jerked to her side as fast as her head snapped left. "He still won't drink. He keeps rambling about saving me."

"Looks like he did." The holy man was unconscious but breathing shallow and rapid.

"Fuck you, Nick. He said he would drink if I prayed with him. I did it just to get him to drink. He gave me this." A gold cross and chain hung down from her index finger. "Here, you take it. I don't need this thing, and I'm not wearing it!"

"I don't have any pockets." I took off my hat to avoid breaking the chain.

The old man started coughing and spit up some black bile. Beth caressed his head while wiping away sweat and vomit. She'd witnessed many patients' last breaths. She knew the end was near. "There, Father. You rest now. You rest." She stroked his head while he gasped for each breath. He tried to speak, but fluids blocked his vocal cords, a gurgling sound was best he could produce. "You rest. I'll do it, Father." She drew a breath. "Our Father, who art in heaven, hallow be thy name..."

I was speechless. I'd never heard Beth pray before. *What did those two talk about while I was down in the ditch?* "...Thy kingdom come, Thy will be done..." I kept up with Beth. She never faltered, but did not cross her forehead, only looked at her watch. She slipped out from under the body. There was nothing soft to place under his head.

Her watch hit the pavement causing a small spark. "No sense carrying around dead weight. Can you believe I checked for the exact time of death? Old habit."

Her demeanor didn't surprise me. She had been desensitized. We were on our way again. The handles of the wagons squeaked as we continued south.

I wanted to ask Beth what they talked about while I was gone, but couldn't find the courage. So we walked silently.

Underpasses turned out to be obstacles, because everyone took cover under them. People crashed their cars into others under the bridge, just to get away from the molten rain. They drove up and around the guardrails to get under the overpass to the point that we couldn't get by without climbing over one or two burned vehicles. Several times we emptied the wagons to portage the dam of wrecked cars.

Most of the fires were out, but still smoldering. We tried to stay upwind of every fire we saw. Our lungs were fried and we didn't need any more chemicals in them than we already had. Some of the trucks made me nervous. There was no way to know what they were carrying.

We came across an armored car. In an attempt to escape the flames the guard had opened his door, and it remained unlocked. The keys still hung on his belt, or what was left of it. "Here's our chance, babe. All we got to do is take all the money out, hide it in the woods, and come back and get it when this whole thing is over, we'll be set."

Beth's response came quickly. "Do you really think money is going to be worth anything anymore? We've gone back to the barter system. The question is: will there be anybody to barter with?"

We opted not to waste precious energy retrieving something that was now obsolete.

The sound of water alerted us to yet another culvert. I scampered down the embankment like I had for every culvert or tunnel we'd come across.

The water trickled out ankle deep. Tree roots and other branches blocked the entrance. The only way to see to the other side required kneeling on all fours. Some of the debris seemed loose enough to pull out. Setting it aside, I poked the torch and my head into the drainage pipe. Too small for anybody other than a small child, this one was empty too.

I was about to back out and head up to Beth, when something came out of the pile of debris. It hissed and growled as it scampered towards me. I screamed like a schoolgirl. I jerked myself out of the culvert banging my head on the edge and cutting my forehead slightly. I continued to stumble while climbing up to the road. My feet couldn't move fast enough, expecting to get bit from behind with every missed step.

"What's wrong with you?" Beth asked.

"There's a fucking possum in that culvert. Scared the shit out of me!" And to think I handled them for a living, or at least used to.

From the light of the torch Beth could see blood coming down my forehead. She put her hand in my pocket and tore out the remaining material. She quickly tended to the bleeding while she laughed. A rare thing lately, so I took the chiding along with the nursing.

Once my heart slowed to a normal pace we resumed our trek to the city. Our last torch went out. With nothing to relight it, we traveled in the dark again.

I was hoping I would hear sirens or something the closer we got. Silence was the only sound we heard when we stopped walking to listen. Not even the hint of a breeze could be felt.

Silence is an eerie sound. The only time I ever remember hearing silence, was ice fishing up north, and we were far from land. Even then it only lasted a short time, but it didn't take long until I questioned my ability to hear. I'd strain to pick up the faintest sound. Then I'd find myself clapping my hands, or going, "Woo, woo, woo," so I'd know I hadn't gone deaf. Eventually a plane or snowmobile would break the stillness and I'd take a breath again.

There was no talking between us. We continued on towards the city. The only sound was our shoes on the blistered blacktop. I noticed that we timed it so that we would only be making the noise of one person walking. We both knew it, but neither one of us changed a step, keeping our thoughts to ourselves. Her thoughts were surely of her children, and grandchildren. They weren't actually my grandbabies, but they thought they were. They called me "Papa."

I figured with no light she couldn't see my face, so I asked, "I noticed you praying earlier. What did you two talk about?"

"I kept trying to make him drink, but he wouldn't until he finished his story. Something about Sodom and Gomorrah, something about God's covenant. It's all mumbo jumbo to me."

"Wait. I saw you praying, and I heard you recite the Lord's Prayer without missing a beat."

"First, I wasn't praying. He asked me to hold my hands that way, so he could give me the cross. Second, I said a prayer familiar to all Christians to comfort my patient. I can recite the Shema in Hebrew too if you like. Making the patient comfortable at the time of death just seems the right thing to do. It's just part of a good bedside manner."

"So he didn't save you, did he?"

"I didn't need saving. You saved me."

The first day on the interstate was long and we stopped when we found a cement building at a sub station of a power terminal. The hatchet made little work of the locked door.

We went without a fire or light that night. It was good to feel a breeze. It was still hot, like that trip we spent in Vegas in July, around one hundred to one hundred and fifteen degrees. Even though it was difficult to see, we needed a respite from the heat. Plus, I didn't think there was much left in the dark to be afraid of.

We lay down on the cement floor with no pillows. Neither one of us complained.

Chapter 10
The Tower

We left the comfort of our dark cement vault once we woke from a much-needed rest. The difference between day and night remained indistinguishable.

"Are you ready for breakfast?" I held up two cans of food. "Remember a day without orange juice is..."

"Just give me the cans." The labels were missing. What Beth thought was beets, was butter beans. The can she guessed contained green beans, held spoiled cranberry sauce, at least we suspected it to be spoiled. We were not taking any chances. There was no doctor to take care of us, no 911 to call. We couldn't afford to get any sicker than we were. I still had diarrhea, but at least Beth was feeling better.

Eating can upon can of cold vegetables only to fill the hole took all the pleasure out of eating. Straight butter beans are not a good way to start the day, but we packed as much into our bellies as we could before the long walk. Phony Bologna and eggs would have been appreciated for once.

Again we were bound for Syracuse. We didn't get a hundred yards when Beth stopped walking. "I'm getting so sick of hearing these wheels. Let's ditch these wagons. We'll take soda and just a few cans of food, we'll carry it in the pack, and we can move faster. There's bound to be places where we can get food when we get there. They'll probably have supplies and shelters set up for the survivors. Hopefully we can get some news on what happened and find out what friggin' time it is."

We brought the wagons back to the building and moved much faster without them.

After what seemed like hours, Beth broke the silence. "We must be getting close to people soon. It's been three lanes for some time now. We should have seen some sign of life, don't you think? Fires, sounds or something. The whole city can't be dead, can it?"

She was looking in the wrong places again. She expected them to be lined up along the exit ramps. No, we would find people near the remains of super-markets, or where we could find fresh water.

It was storming in the south, and occasionally the silhouette of a water tower could be seen in the distance when lightning flashed. The wind picked up, and ashes started to swirl about. The panorama reminded me of a scene from H.G. Well's book, "War of the Worlds," the area totally devastated, with the Martian machine looking over its accomplishments.

"That's where we can get some fresh water," I said, but didn't know how just yet.

We had to leave the interstate and cross a bridge. I looked down into the water and saw about fifteen or twenty bodies surrounded by dead fish of varying sizes. The fish didn't make it either because of all the soot and ash in the water. A thick film rested on the surface, broken only where rats swam through; there were hundreds of them scurrying on the bank.

Every flash of lightning gave a different perspective.

The bodies were bloated, but only the part sticking out of the water was burned, all black, except their spines, collarbones and skulls. Several conjoined flashes of lightning revealed the total horror. Every one of them drowned. They'd stayed under as long as they could. When they poked their heads up to breath, they were met with searing hot air and ash, the exact scenario the father and his daughters experienced. It was the same at nearly every bridge we crossed.

The lightning made it easy to head towards the water tower. We didn't need to stick to the streets. We could walk around the cellars and cut cross lots, dodging the remains of buildings and automobiles.

The tower was the highest thing left standing in that area. We could see what was left of some of the taller buildings down closer to the center of the city, but the skyline was very different than I remembered it. The earthquake had leveled the tallest buildings, the fires lowered the rest.

We only had a couple of blocks to go to get to the tower. I thought we would have spotted a fire or some torches the closer we got. We saw nothing.

"I'm going to try and get us some clean water. You stay here and see if you can find cloth for more torches." I had been gathering old crusty grease along the way, but the only clothing we had found was on bodies, and I couldn't go through that again. "Make sure you stay within shouting distance. We don't want to lose each other."

The storm intensified, and seeing was no longer an issue. The tower loomed on a hill, back dropped by clouds linked together by ribbons of lightning. Thunder claps never had a rest between each other.

In the past, Beth and I would sit outside to watch a summer storm, kind of romantic. This storm radiated a more ominous emotion, eerie, like something from a Stephen King novel.

I turned several times to make sure I could still see Beth. She was wandering near the river.

The climb was exhausting. When I approached the base of the tower it was clear a building once stood before the fire, but the debris seemed placed along the edges revealing a path. Once I made it to the base, I could see a big pipe wrench on the piping leading from the tower.

Somebody had taken these pipes apart to get water. "There are survivors," I said.

I quickly turned and ran to tell Beth the good news. "Forget the cloth," I yelled. "People..., people have been here. Come up here, hurry up." I doubt that she understood anything I said.

I could see her coming up the hill. She yelled something inaudible as she ran.

This time I was going to wait for her to get closer. I didn't feel like repeating myself. My constant diarrhea and vomiting had weakened me, and I knew she wouldn't be able to understand me anyways.

"What did you say? Did you see somebody alive?" Then she said something I couldn't understand. She kept asking questions all the way up the hill. She was really getting pissed that I wasn't answering her back. "Will you answer me, damn it?" She finally made it to the top of the hill. She was too out of breath to ask any more questions. "What... you. What..." She grabbed all the air left in her lungs and squeezed out, "Talk to me, asshole." She threw down some clothing she found.

"There are people here. They got water out of the tower. Somebody's survived. We're looking for them. They can't be far. They wouldn't leave water too far behind. We've got to find supermarkets. That's where we'll find them. Let's move now, babe." We would find people soon.

"So you don't need any of this?" She picked up a handful of clothing. A small child's dress still dripped with water from the river.

As for potable water, all we had to do is help ourselves. The wrench was there for our convenience. There was a bucket and everything.

I cracked the coupling enough to let water run in the bucket. When I was sure the water was clean, I put a ladle that somebody left here for anybody to use, in the dripping water. With only the light from lightning, I looked to see if there was any dirt in the water. It was warm, and tasted funny, but Beth and I drank until we got cramps.

Neither one of us had washed since we left the culvert. We stripped and washed off layers of soot, blood, and just plain filth. We washed without soap.

I had watched Beth shower a million times before. This time was different. Her hair was nearly gone. Each time she ran her hands over her head large fistfuls of hair came out. I saw her burns. Each crevice appeared to have second or third degree burns. Her body still had the curves that ancient Romans found voluptuous and sexual. I can understand why they painted so many naked chubby chicks. I was never turned on by those skinny model types. I had a funny feeling that I had better learn to adapt.

We washed our clothes and put them back on wet. We were ready to go.

It seemed like a long walk to where the supermarkets were. It was never that long when we drove. The hills seemed a lot steeper too. I guess I never paid attention to them before.

I had to stop a couple of times to let my stomach settle down a bit. My guts were all torn up inside.

We came to the shopping centers. The big signs to the malls were still there. The plastic had melted and was hanging down like stalactites in a cave, leaving the skeletons of their framework exposed.

We entered the parking lot. One by one, we passed shells of vehicles I couldn't identify. I can only imagine the heat given off when all these cars, trucks, motorcycles were burning at the same time.

Even though there were no fires left burning, the air had the acrid smell of burned rubber.

In my mind's eye, I could still see other shoppers going between parked cars and trucks, carrying packages. This landscape was eerily silent and void of life. Many of the light poles had melted from the heat of the vehicles parked next to them, and collapsed. I'm sure they were fabricated from some cheaply made aluminum alloy, not intended for strength or durability.

Portions of the mall itself were still standing, or at least the cement block walls and some of the iron girders were still standing. We headed around the corner towards the back entrance. We weren't looking for food, we were looking for people, and then we saw the fire. This wasn't a fire left over from the mall fire. This was one made just recently, by people. We could see them in the distance, walking around it.

Chapter 11
A Cold Reception

"Come on." I grabbed Beth by the arm and we started to run. "Hello, hello. Over here. Hello."

Two men got up and ran towards us. A large black man holding a big pipe as a weapon yelled in a slow deep voice, "Get on back now."

We stopped in our tracks.

Another man shrieked in a southern accent, "Git back, git away, git out of here. We don't want you here. Git, go on, leave us alone."

Another man walked up behind the first two and didn't say a word. The first two came at us in a threating manner. The third one was calmer. I could tell he was the one in charge.

"We're just looking for some help, some food, and water, and shelter." I tried to reason with the third one, looking him straight in the eye.

The lanky one said, "There ain't nuthin' left here, they took too much already. Now git out of here." The pitch in his trembling voice rose at the end of his last command. It was obvious that he wasn't anyone to be afraid of. His voice cracked as he pretended to be a bigger man than he really was.

The little man's tirade was interrupted by the one in charge. "Shut up, Tex, you've said too much already." He walked closer to greet us. "They're nothing to worry about." As soon as he spoke, the other two dropped their guards and became docile.

"My name's Nick and this is Beth." I didn't think last names were important right now. "We're from upstate. We came down along the interstate. How many of you are there?

Without any introduction he spoke. "First things first. I run this place and I decide what questions will be asked and I'll be the one asking them. Secondly, I'm sorry but there's not enough food for everyone so I'm going to have to ask you to leave, but before you do, we'll give you one meal, and all the water you can carry, and then you'll have to go. Don't come back. Fair enough?" He came forward like this was a business deal and he was in a rush to meet a deadline.

"Yea... ok ... " I was still in shock. This was not the welcome wagon I was expecting. I expected that people would want us to join their group of survivors—strength in numbers. "We're no threat to you. We just thought if we could find a group of people, we all would have a better chance of surviving. Beth's a nurse and maybe she could help with..."

"We've got that all solved," he interrupted. "Look, here's how it is. We had enough food up until two days ago. We had some stolen. We would have let you both stay then, but now there's not enough. Giving away one meal to everyone that passes by is more than the rest of the group would like, but that's the best we can do. You probably won't like what we have to feed you either. They won't let me give away any of the good food. You're going to get the stuff nobody else wants."

I could sense the pressure he felt, but believed he still held the authority of the group. "Well, we'll take whatever you offer. Thank you."

Beth and I walked behind the third guy as he headed back to the rest. He hadn't even told us his name.

I kept looking over my shoulder at the scrawny guy. I positioned Beth in front of me. I didn't like the way he acted. I half expected to get hit in the back of the head as he followed us. He just had a weasel-looking face. I didn't trust him.

We walked over to the fire smoldering under a small section of roof that had survived the earthquake. Two people got up so we could sit down. All it took was a hand gesture from their leader. I felt very unwelcome and anxious. Nobody said a word until we both sat down on some cement blocks that were placed in a circle, like campfires when we used to go camping. I thought for sure that somebody would break out a guitar and start playing "Kumbaya."

"Have you seen any other people or any other animals alive?" He didn't waste any time asking the questions he promised he would.

"We've seen a lot of rats, an opossum, and a priest who died soon after we found him. Other than that, we haven't even seen a dog." I had said enough and stopped giving any more free information until he made it worth our while.

"Have you found any place that didn't burn?"

"Would we be here if we did?" I said, and then realized that I back talked to him. We were really in no position to piss these people off. "No, I'm sorry. It's been horrible for us. Beth lost her family, we lost our house and..."

It was Beth's turn to interrupt me. "Nick, they don't care." She surprised me when she spoke up.

"That's right honey, we all lost people. Your people weren't any better than our families." Some middle-aged African American woman with no teeth blurted out, and then raised her voice. "And who gives you the right...?"

The leader broke in to what was sure to be a confrontation. "Bonita, shhhh baby, be quiet."

Instantly she quieted down and went back to fiddling with the fire. This guy really did have command of the group.

"My name's Mick. Hi, Nick."

I reached out my hand to shake his. "Mick."

To my surprise, he reached out his hand and said, "Nick."

We all gave a very subtle and muffled chuckle. No one dared laugh out loud. It wasn't time yet.

He seemed like an intelligent man, quick witted and apparently accustomed to dealing with people. There was a nametag on his shirt, but it didn't tell where he had worked. Though balding, he didn't try to hide it with a comb over, but yet still had more hair than Beth.

"Just how many people do you think there are still alive in the city?" I felt I had gained his trust enough to ask a question.

He gazed in my direction awhile then said, "You're lucky I like you." He pressed his lips together. "I really can't be sure. We have pretty much stayed here protecting this store. We put a claim on everything here, and the only way to keep it to ourselves is to stay here. There've been a few small groups passing through. We ran a couple of them off. We fed some and then sent them on their way. There's only enough food left here for us." He shook and rubbed his head. "Nobody has claimed the water tower. I'm sure someone will take it hostage and only give water for food. We'd do it but we don't have any guns, and none of us has the nerve to defend it. For now, it's still run by the city. Just turn the pipe wrench to the left and catch it when it starts to drip, then turn it to the right to stop it from leaking out. There's no way to fill it back up. When it's gone we'll drink what we can find. Wait a minute. I thought I was supposed to be asking the questions. Do you have anything to carry water in?"

"I guess I could poke a couple of holes in a can and then plug the holes with a screw or something." I didn't have anything but we had to keep hydrated in this heat. Even though it was dark all the time, it was constantly muggy. The heat drained us of all energy. We sweated from the time we crawled out of that tunnel and about five minutes after we washed up.

"I'm going to give each of you a going away gift. I shop at Gander Mountain." He motioned with a drinking motion to a young boy crouching adjacent to the fire. "Marcos, bring me two canteens."

The little guy jumped up as soon as he was asked. Apparently he was the keeper of the canteens. "Can I have some candy now?" He turned to look at our host.

"Give one to each of them, and then come here," Mick said.

Off he scampered into the darkness, to return within less than two minutes, stirring up a
plume of ashes as he skidded to a stop in front of
Mick.

"Give one to each of our new friends."

The little guy came over to Beth first, handed
over a blackened and dented canteen, looked her
in the eyes, and said, "Don't worry; your hair will
grow back."

Beth looked down at her feet. Her hair was
so important to her. I'd spent many hours comb-
ing my fingers through it. When it started to turn
grey, she went to the salon religiously, every two
weeks, to get it colored back to its original hue.
"Thank you," she said.

He handed me another. "Thank you," I said.

The youngster turned away towards Mick,
and the light of the fire reflected off his barc skin.
The tops of his shoulders were covered with sores
that seemed to be draining. Some of the material of his shirt had melted into his skin. He didn't
seem to be very uncomfortable considering his
burns. I didn't comment.

I looked at Mick with sincerity and said,
"Thank you very, very much Mick. I know how
valuable these are." I held up the canteen, metal
with a metal cap. You could tell both had gone
through the fire. Mine was discolored, dented,
and the cap was loose and probably leaked.

"They all leak," Mick said, "but if you wrap a small piece of cloth around the top, it'll be the same as the rubber gasket that burned out."

"You've got candy?" I didn't mean to blurt it out quite like that, but I couldn't imagine how something made out of almost one hundred percent sugar, made it through the fires. I've seen marshmallows burn.

Mick looked up at me. "Power has its privileges, and right now it's a currency that works, among others." He reached into a pocket on each side of his jacket and pulled something out with each hand. He handed the candy to the little burned guy, who quickly ran over to where he was sitting before he was summoned up.

When the little guy tried to sit down again, the pains of his burns were now visible on his face. He put a piece of what I thought was candy into his mouth. Tears ran down his cheek as he tried to smile, but the smile lost out to a pursed upper lip.

A woman wearing a pair of men's work boots that were obviously too big, gave him a canteen. He drank the water and threw his head back as if he had taken a pill.

He put the cap back on and handed the canteen back.

Without a word, the woman motioned with one hand for the boy to finish all the water. Understanding her sign language, he complied. This time when he handed the empty container off, it was accepted without a word. The woman turned and went back to her cinderblock seat, to continue her silent stare into the only light around.

The youngster put something else into his mouth, tossing it from one cheek to the other with his tongue. This time the smile came back, but it was crisscrossed with muddy streaks of tears.

Now I understood why he seemed free of pain. "Where did you find the pain killers?" Had my question crossed a line?

"Shhh." Mick stood up, motioned with his head, and said, "Let's go for a walk."

I followed him to the edge of one of the remaining walls. Either he trusted me or he was going to kill me. We stopped when we were out of hearing range of the rest of the survivors.

Mick looked over towards the group as if searching for one particular individual. He seemed very apprehensive. "You see, there was once this pharmacist who thought he had a failsafe plan to retire early. He and his partner could move out of the city. Retire in some old farmhouse, someplace quiet, someplace more tolerant." He stopped to wipe his eyes and nose with his sleeve. Taking a deep breath he continued. "So... this pharmacist deposited the sweepings of ineptness away into a safe every once in a while. Management was so lax about record keeping that as long as they didn't change managers, I had it made. In about two more years I was going to unload everything all at once, take the money and run. Then this happened. I knew I would never retire." He shook his head. He was taking this whole thing personal.

"You're going to need that stuff now, more than ever. Why are you telling me about it? If I were you, I would keep quiet about it and use it on the people that need it." I didn't feel comfortable knowing about his stash. If the wrong people found out about his safe, things could get chaotic.

"Yes I know. I've been giving them to whomever needs them. I'm afraid in doing so, word has spread about my little clinic. That's why I'm confiding in you. I need somebody on my side, somebody I can trust... I can trust you, can't I, Nick? I need somebody."

I wasn't ready to pledge allegiance to anybody yet. "What about those two guys that threatened us. They seemed pretty loyal. They were ready to kill for you."

"Those guys were just trying to scare you away because the rest of the group didn't want any more food given away to strangers. The big guy, Carl, he wouldn't hurt a fly. He was a conductor on the monorail. He recognized what was going on and stopped the train underground. He led twenty-three people into a maintenance tunnel. He led six out. The rest of them died of asphyxiation.

Three more died before they made it here. Now Tex, I wouldn't trust him as far as I could throw him. He has a cowboy hat and talks with a fake southern accent, pretends to be a real tough guy. I think he's from New Jersey."

Mick turned back to look at the group. "He was on Carl's train. Carl told me that when they were in the maintenance tunnel, he saw the asshole push some children away from a crack in the wall, where breathable air was coming in. Carl wanted to stop him, but he was busy rotating children and the elderly so they could breathe near a ventilation shaft. The kids didn't make it, Tex did. We only let him stick around because he's good at scavenging around in the debris, like the rat he is. He has found a lot of food for everyone, but he makes sure that he gets the best of it all. That's the only reason he's doing it. He's the reason I'm talking to you. He seems extremely interested in what I have in my left pocket. Another thing, he's gone way too long when he goes scavenging. Sometimes he comes back with nothing. Other times he comes back with things, but won't tell where he found them. I don't trust him.

Will you and your woman stick by me, so I can talk these people into leaving this mall and looking for more survivors? As it stands, Bonita has a lot of pull with the rest them. They won't leave the place because Bonita wants to stay. I guess she just yells louder. I have some control of her because I keep her sedated. She won't let Marcos leave, and I won't go because he needs these pills. If I left them with Marcos, Tex would take them away, then Marcos would suffer." Again he nervously looked back at the rest.

I felt extremely uncomfortable. "I'm sure that Beth wants to go down to the hospital and see if she can help out." I scrambled for any excuse, since staying here wouldn't increase our odds of survival.

"Let's go back to the fire, and we'll get something into your stomach," Mick said.

We made it back to the fire after stumbling on broken cement blocks and other debris.

There was a large slab of Phony Bologna on a makeshift grate. It looked burned, as if it had been there for a while.

Mick saw me looking at it and handed us both a plate and fork and knife. "Enjoy this. It'll probably be the last meat you'll eat for a long time. We're using up the last of it. Most of it is rancid, but when it's cooked well done, it's edible. Until somebody gets sick we're going to eat it all, then we'll hit the canned goods. We found some seasonings. Those take away the spoiled taste... kind of."

"You still didn't tell me how many people are left alive in the city. Aren't there any shelters?"

These people already made it clear that we would only be welcome one night. Tomorrow we would still need water and food. The water that we could carry in the canteens would only last us a day if we rationed it. We'd need to drink twice that much every day.

Carl spoke up. "Ain't one shelter in the city that was prepared for this. All of them burned to the ground. They were designed for the cold, ya know? Three hots and a cot, out of the cold, off the street. We've all been there once... well maybe not all of us." He looked at Beth and me, and then at Beth's diamond ring. The fire reflected off it still, though it was covered in soot and dirt.

Again I felt threatened here. I noticed Tex looking at her hand. I knew Beth did too. I knew money wasn't worth anything anymore, but gems never lose their value, in one way or the other. These might get us a couple cans of soup, who knows, they might be worth even more in the future.

Chapter 12
On the Road Again

Beth and I slept away from the others. I awoke to see a figure looming over her while she rested.

I leapt to my feet. "What to fuck! Get to fuck away from her!" I lunged at the man as he dodged my grasp. He ran off away from the area and into the dark. "Get back here you son of a bitch!" Chasing after him and leaving Beth alone was something I wouldn't do.

"What's going on?" Mick asked as he rose.

Beth was awake too. First thing she did was look for her ring. "What was he doing?"

"It was that guy with the cowboy hat. He was hanging over my wife. That motherfucker better not show his ass back here again. I'll kill him!" My heart felt like it would come out of my chest. I sank to the ground, even though a cement block was within my reach. I didn't think I could balance myself on one.

"Tex. I knew he was trouble. I hope he doesn't come back. We'll do our own scavenging," Mick said.

Bonita, Marcos, and Carl came over and stood near Beth. The more vocal of the three reminded, "It's time for you to leave now anyways. We fed you, and now it's time to go. You said you would leave in the morning. That's what you said, Mick."

"I'm sorry, Nick. She's right, but I did say one meal. We will, however, give you a few cans of food so you can have breakfast. But then we will be forced to ask you to leave. May God be with you."

"Great," Beth muttered.

Carl looked at his watch and said, "They can have them for supper."

"What do you mean?" I asked. "What time is it? I just assumed we all went to sleep because it was night."

Carl pushed the button to light up the face again. "It's 5:30 p.m."

Beth and I looked at each other. Then she asked Carl, "What day is this?"

"I don't know how to bring that up, I just use it to tell time, but today is Thursday."

"You wouldn't want to part with your watch would you, Carl?"

"What do you have to trade for it?" He pointed to her ring.

"Oh, no way! I don't need to know what time it is that bad. What difference does it make now anyway?" She hid her hand under her folded arms.

Mick motioned to Marcos. "Go get four cans out of the pile without labels, and try not to get any that are dented."

Again the little guy took off running.

Beth helped me with the backpack. She unstuck the tape for me as I put it on. "We need to get something for the torches," she whispered.

"Mick, is there any clothing we can use for the torches?" I asked.

"Not much at all. You've seen what there is."

Bonita started in again. "No, you didn't say anything about giving away anything but one meal. You already told Marcos to give them the good stuff. Give them the dented cans. What have they done for us?"

"Come on, Nick. We better get going." Beth took my arm and we both turned to walk away.

Marcos yelled, "Wait, wait. Don't go yet. You forgot your food!"

Beth thanked him and put the cans in my pack. We walked off into the darkness, in the opposite direction Tex had, back to the water tower.

Except for our brand new canteens, the empty cans I'd made into containers, and six cans of mystery food, we were traveling light. The weight carried by each of us would increase once we loaded up with water.

I was worried about somebody guarding the tower. "Maybe you better take off your ring before we get up there."

"They'll have to break my fucking finger off, but they'll be doing it without any nuts," she snapped.

I said nothing more about the subject.

When we reached the top of the hill there was no one to greet us. "Now what do we do?" she asked.

It's clean water. Drink as much as you can. No telling when we'll get our next fresh clean drink. Be careful not to step on a nail. We can't afford any injuries now."

"No, I was talking about after we get the water."

I didn't have an answer. We had about two days of water and four cans of food.

"What do you want to do? You're driving." I looked at her and realized that I shouldn't have said it.

Once in a while, Beth and I would hop into one of our vehicles and let the wind take us where ever it blew. It usually depended on who was driving at the time as to where we went, or what we did. Of course if I was driving I would go into the mountains and look for wildlife, and silence.

Of course if she was driving we would head down to the casino. She loved to gamble and so did her son. Those were some of our best times.

I have stuck my foot in my mouth before, just like everyone else has, but this was devastating. I realized it at the same time she did.

We just held each other and wept. We wept hard and long, making almost no sounds. Neither one of us wanted to break the silence that I was starting to hate.

We drank as much water as our guts would hold, and then we filled the canteens and soup cans. We bathed ourselves with some of the city's remaining drinking water, even though Mick had asked us not to. Beth would not give on that.

We decided to look in individual houses instead of hanging around shopping centers. It seemed to be the safer course to take, even though we were searching in the dark. After going without light for so long, our eyes grew accustomed. We had to be careful what we salvaged because we could only carry so much. Water was the most important thing, but at about eight pounds a gallon, we had to think of a way to find it, instead of carrying it. The heat was too intense to go without it long. All the rivers, streams, and brooks were filled with either sooty sludge or something dead. There was no electricity to run water pumps, and most, if not all, of the pipes under the streets were twisted and broken because of the earthquake. There was no water except for the tower that we felt safe drinking, but I didn't feel safe there, and neither did Beth. I think mostly because of what Mick said about somebody taking the tower for ransom. I was sure it would happen sooner or later.

"I wonder if any cars made it inside parking garages." I was really getting sick of walking. I'd always said we should walk or get more exercise. Now I would take a ride on anything. I was really getting tired. The constant diarrhea had weakened me.

"There's one at the hospital and one at the dome." She came down to the city a lot more than I did. "I know there're a couple more on the east side of town."

"Which is closer, the hospital or the dome?"

"I'm not sure. Everything is confusing me. Half of the buildings are gone. Nothing looks the same. We have to find a street sign. I think the hospital is closer if we go this way and cut across lots. We might find a shelter there."

I almost said the old, "You're driving," thing, but I caught myself this time. "Good idea. How much further do you think it is as the crow flies?"

As she was doing the calculations in her head, I realized that even the English language was going to change if we continued to exist. Would anyone ever see a crow fly again?

"It can't be more than a mile, but we'll have to climb up an overpass or two. I'm not sure; it's so hard to tell." She pointed towards where she thought the hospital was. Every time she would think about an overpass she would raise her hand up, and then down, like her hand had to go up and over an imagined overpass.

"How much water do you have left?" We'd had a canteen, and a two-quart soup can of water each when we started. We were drinking out of the canteens first. It was just more convenient. The soup cans had a hole in the top plugged with some cloth bunched up tight like a cork in a wine bottle.

"My can's still full but I don't have much left in my canteen," she said as she opened it and downed the rest. "Correction, my canteen's empty."

I had to take off my half-assed backpack to get my can out. The tape kept sticking to my shirt, but with enough struggling, I got the pack off. I was careful not to tip it over, but when I found the can, the cloth plug had come out. I hadn't noticed the water running down my back because I was already soaked with sweat, and the water was as warm as we were. "Argh…" I growled. "We need to find a way to get some water now. My can's almost empty. The plug came out. I didn't think this would work. C'mon, babe, think. We need to put our heads together and work as a team. We're all alone in this world." I never, ever, ever, ever thought that I would use that cliché, and have it be so true.

"If it starts to rain we can catch it. We can boil water to sterilize it. I even heard a guy tell another guy at work, you can drink your own urine as long as you strain it through your sock. I'm not straining it through your sock though. What about water heaters down in people's cellars?" That was the end of the fooling around. She was back to business. I was glad, too. She was the brains of our team. As long as she was with me we could lick any problem.

"A lot of them were crushed when the bulk of the buildings fell. Plus you can't get at the drains at the bottom. There's too much debris. Then if you can, it's melted shut. I checked seven or eight different places before we hit the throughway when I was scouting."

"What about radiators in cars?"

The poor girl, she could tell you what Einstein meant when he formulated the equation $E=mc2$. She could tell you about the cosmos, evolution, paleontology, medicine, anything science, but I'll be dammed, she knew nothing about vehicles, balancing a budget, or doing the grocery shopping. When the bills needed paying, even though we had the money, if I didn't pay them, they didn't get paid. When we first got married, she had an SUV. She kept driving that rig until one day it just quit. She had actually blown the engine in a vehicle, only because she never checked the oil. I think it's important to know the arts and music, math and science, history, sports. It's all important. There's a thing called good old-fashioned common sense. I was never taught that in school. That was taught to me by my dad and uncles and grandfather. They're the ones that taught me engines don't run without oil, your dog will not live without water, righty tighty, lefty loosey, and some things that my grandpa told me not to repeat.

"Hello, what about radiators in cars?" she yelled at me. She gets irate when I don't answer her right away.

"They all have antifreeze in them, babe. Keep thinking." That's when I started thinking. Would there be any oil left in the block of a car, after it has burned like these have? If so, we could use it for the torches. It would be hard to check a car, since they were too low to the ground because the tires burned off. Trucks had bigger clearances, and held more oil, but we'd need bigger tools to pull the plug. I needed to find a big adjustable wrench.

"I need a big piece of flashing and two big pots that can take a good fire. We won't die of thirst on my shift." She was still thinking of how to get water.

I wasn't all that up on starting a fire unless we had to. Attention is something I like, but only when I'm ready and prepared for it. That was another problem we had to think about. Nearly all the fires were out now. We had to find another way of lighting torches. We couldn't paw around for hot coals anymore. Butane lighters couldn't stand the heat very well. We might find a "Zippo," but there would be no fluid to put in it. We had to think of something, or find something. The cellars were cool enough to look around in, but we'd still have to be careful of nails and such.

"My stomach feels all tore up. We need to take a break, and I'm beat." The constant diarrhea was still being followed by nausea and intolerable cramps.

We both sat down on the ground to rest.

"Give me some of that cloth."

She dug through my backpack, easier than me trying to take it off. She gave me a couple pieces, and I headed off to the side of the street. I found a charred tree trunk to hide behind. Even though Beth and I had been married almost nine years, I still needed privacy sometimes. This was one of those times.

"Do you still have diarrhea?" She yelled.

"Will you shut up?" I said as loud as I could whisper, making sure she could hear, but nobody else could. Then I realized that there was no one around for me to be embarrassed in front of. "Yes I do."

"You know what you have? Beaver fever, it's from that water we drank in that culvert. I'll probably get it too. It's very contagious. From now on we better drink out of our own canteen. Was any of the meat you ate rare?" Being a nurse she knew what questions to ask, but not when to ask them.

"Can you please shut up for a couple of minutes, I'm busy here." I tried to wipe myself, but the friggin' backpack wouldn't let my arms down low enough to reach my butt. Again I struggled with the pack. Some of the tape had rolled over so the sticky side was stuck to my skin. I ended up pulling my whole shirt off. "God damn it!" I didn't care who heard me. I was in the mood to kick anybody's ass. I was standing half bent over with shit hanging out my ass. Concerned that it might land on my feet, or pants, I was afraid to stand up. To add insult to injury, I had lost my wiping cloth in the darkness. Now I had to stand there with nothing on from my ankles up, trying not to step in my own shit, trying to fish more cloth out of my sticky backpack, just so I could wipe my ass. "Aaaarrrrgggggg." I growled like a bear, I was so fucking mad.

I finally got myself pulled together and stepped around the tree.

"You don't remember eating anything rotten that I didn't eat, do you?" Nurse Beth asked. "Other than canned food, we both ate the same beef at Mick's. It did taste tainted, but look at what it's been through. I don't think it was too bad to eat. It was definitely well done, more like jerky. I think you'll be ok as long as you don't get worse. Yup, I think you have Beaver Fever; it comes from the parasites that are found in the water that we drank when we were in the tunnel."

"I heard you the first time." I wasn't in the mood for another one of her science lectures. She would always try to start up conversations about science and other things that I didn't know about, or honestly, care about. Not to make me feel stupid, but just because she was so interested in the subjects that she had to talk about it to somebody. It was usually a one sided conversation. I got used to them after a while. Sometimes I even listened. Right now I wasn't in the mood.

"You know, if we were smart, we would have climbed the tower to look for fires in the distance," she said.

"Well you're the smart one. Let's go back and you can climb up." My stomach just wasn't into it. "If you want to know the truth, I would like to make camp, gather our thoughts, and maybe some food."

"Do you think you can make it to the hospital?" she asked.

"Yes, I suppose that would be our best plan." I put my backpack back on and we began our trek again. I had to stop speaking because I was getting painful cramps again. I was in too much pain to be angry. Climbing up to the highway near an overpass took all the energy I could muster. I was hoping to see some sign of life once we got up higher on the road, but all we could see was darkness. There were no fires visible.

After about an hour of walking I couldn't take any more. "I've got to stop again. Damn it. How long will I be sick like this?" I took off my sticky pack, dug out the last bit of cloth we were going to use for torch, and looked for a private place to do my business. "Are you sure that we're going the right way?"

There was a long pause. That's when I knew she wasn't sure herself.

"Yes," she said, followed by another long pause. "Hey, look there. Look over there. There's a light or something."

I twisted to look around the remaining trunk of the tree, my pants down to my ankles. I couldn't stop what I had started doing, but I could hurry it along. Cleaning up to the best of my ability, I pulled up my pants and quickly looked around the burned skeleton of the tree. I saw nothing. Now I couldn't see Beth either. "Hey where did you go? Beth...Beth."

Chapter 13
Refugees

Panic gripped me and I ran to where she had been. "Beth, Beth, where to hell did you go?" I yelled.

"Quiet, down here. Look over there. I thought I saw a light, but now it's gone." She was looking out into the distance, her right hand over her forehead, as if she was shielding her eyes from the sun, all I could see was the silhouette of her body against the dim light that was leaking through the clouds.

"Why are you doing that? There's no sun." I should have been looking myself, but the idea of her shielding her eyes when there was no sunshine, struck me as odd. Then I turned my attentions towards the direction that she was looking. "I don't see anything." I opened my eyes wide, looked as hard as I could, hoping to find signs of other people. Maybe this time they would be more cooperative. I caught myself raising my right hand up to my forehead. "I don't see anything. I think your hallucinating. You probably caught beaver fever from me." Briefly I thought I saw a flicker of light, similar to when I saw the flash on the first day, but I couldn't be sure. It wasn't a fire. There was no glow in the darkness like there was when we saw Mick's fire.

We both just stood there looking in the dark.

"There!" We both pointed and spoke simultaneously. The square shape of a window could be seen for a split second. Then it was gone.

"Down that way." I pointed in the darkness. "They're down by what's left of those brick buildings we passed." A second or two went by. "There, there, see it? Somebody's got a flashlight," I whispered. "You stay right up here and wait. I'm going to get closer and see what we're up against. Don't worry. I won't let them know I'm there. I'll be right back." I kissed her and started to head down the embankment.

"Be careful and don't go up to them without me," she power-whispered.

"I'll be right back."

As soon as I reached the bottom of the hill, I lost my sense of direction. There was no horizon to follow. Though it was still dark all the time a subtle difference could be detected between earth and sky. None could be seen here. I had to climb back up to Beth and get my bearings.

"Is that you Nick? What's wrong?" She could hear me before she could see me. She was surprised to see me back so soon.

"I just got turned around. Which way were they?" My shame of losing my direction wasn't as strong as my curiosity.

"I haven't seen any light in a while," she said, still with a whisper.

I couldn't go off in the darkness without Beth. I would never find my way back to her.

We waited up on the highest point of the road, hoping to catch another glimpse of light. Was it possible they passed without our noticing? We saw nothing. We waited silently about a half an hour with no clues to their whereabouts. "How long should we keep looking?" I asked while still looking into the dark, straining to see something, anything.

"Well, let's head down to the hospital. Maybe that's where they're going," she said. Beth knew a lot of people down there. She used to work in the city, but the constant waste of life within the gangs, and all the people who lived in the same area as the gangs, drove her to a smaller hospital. She always thought she was a lesser nurse because she couldn't handle the pressure of the city. I think she just got tired of fighting a losing battle. She told me about some kid she had treated several times before, for either gunshot wounds, or punctures. He came in one day with his throat sliced from ear to ear. She turned in her resignation later that day.

"Listen," I whispered. "Can you hear that?" I wasn't sure, but I thought I could hear footsteps coming our way. It had been so quiet that I thought I was imagining it.

"Shhhh." She heard it too.

That pissed me off. I told her to listen and then she tells me to shush. I'd told her to be quiet first.

I could hear the footsteps, but I couldn't see any light. They obviously were coming closer.

Again I whispered, "C'mon let's hide over here." As I looked for a place to hang back and observe who was coming, I was also looking for something to use as a weapon. A pipe or something to use as a club would be fine. I had a knife, a hatchet and a multi-tool, but I needed something to protect her from several people. There was nothing around like a club. I took out the knife and held the hatchet in the other hand.

We hid in the darkness for what felt like a long time, but in reality was only a few minutes. The closer they got the uneasier I became.

"Here take this just in case you need it." I handed the multi-tool to her with the biggest blade out.

We heard a baby cry. Simultaneously we put our weapons away and scrambled to our feet, we climbed down the hill, looking for light, listening for sound.

The baby kept crying and it wasn't long until we had their location pinpointed.

"Let's go on up ahead and meet them as they come over the bridge." I felt like a cowboy ready to cut them off at the pass. Then I remembered Tex.

We scrambled along the side until we came to the area where we thought they would cross.

We could still hear the baby crying. I was letting my guard down. Anybody who had a baby would welcome a nurse into his or her party.

That's when we saw them turn on their flashlight.

I could tell that they were no danger to us. There were a couple of women, with four children, No men that I could tell at first glance.

"Hello, Hello." Beth didn't wait for the okay signal. She just walked a hurried pace down to the other survivors.

She knew what she was doing. I looked over all the people. All I had for light was the flashlight that the head person carried, and that was pointed at Beth. "Hello, I'm a nurse. Can I help with the little ones?" She no longer whispered. Beth wasn't one to be afraid.

The leader with the flashlight, still pointing at Beth, said, "Do you have any water, or food? We have several children and we are no threat to anybody." Both women were carrying a child in each arm. "The children are dehydrated and need help to survive." Her voice trembled. "We came from the hospital."

"Isn't the hospital a shelter in times of crises? What kind of shape is it in?" Beth asked while assisting by taking one child from the woman.

"Lady, I don't know where you've been, but this is more than just a crisis. Those motherfuckers finally went and did it. The hospital would have been a good place to be during a blizzard, hurricane, tornado, or just about anything else. This was a doomsday device that a terrorist detonated. The whole city was burned. It had to be a nuclear bomb. This is worse than any natural disaster. Where's the army or National Guard? Where's any help at all?" A full head of red hair glowed in the beam of the flashlight when she pointed it in her direction. "I think they're eating the corpses already. Please help us, please." The tone of her voice was heightened by anger and frustration.

"It's only me and my husband. I'm Beth, and this is my husband Nick. We're looking for some kind of shelter too. Didn't they set up something at the hospital?"

"The hospital's gone! Everything's gone! Society's gone! The human species is gone! We just came from the hospital! The gangs organized and they have taken over the whole city. They're raping any female age eight to eighty. They're living there and at the dome—what's left of them. We're lucky those bastards let us out with the children. They were tired of all the crying, plus they said the children were eating food that they needed. One guy murdered two of the older people just because they wanted water, and I'm sure they plan to consume their bodies. There are no supplies left anywhere. Please help us. Let's just get to hell away from here!"

Trying to take her mind in a different direction I asked, "Where are they getting their water from?" We needed to refill our canteens soon.

The same woman answered. "They're drinking out of the river now. They're straining it through cloth. Dead bodies and rats are in that water. Cholera is just around the corner. This place is going to be where the new plague starts. We're leaving the city, we don't even know where to go, but we have to get away from here."

The conversation was broken by the cries of a couple children and then the screams of another.

"Did you work at the hospital?" Beth asked.

"Yes, I work in pediatrics. My name's Sarah. This is Maria, we both worked very closely with Dr. Stone."

"Dr. Raymond Stone? I know him. We see each other each year at the conference for the National Downs Syndrome Society in Arkansas. He and I used to..." Again she paused realizing how much life had changed for everyone. I'm sure she was thinking of Sally.

"I knew him." Rapidly she switched from remembering the past to concentrating on the present. "How did you survive with all the children?"

"I could only grab two before we went down into the shelter. It happened so fast. Everybody else was caught up in the evacuation. The top three floors of the hospital collapsed from the earth quake, they didn't see the fire coming." She handed the other baby she was carrying to Beth. "This is Megan and you've been holding Tara. Maria is holding Adam and Eve, at least that's what the gang at the hospital called them... it was some kind of a joke to them...We don't even know what their real names are."

Sarah covered her head with her hands, sat down, and broke down. This was the first time that she could let go of her responsibilities and mourn her own situation.

Beth and I both knew what she was about to go through. We had to face the same irreversible truth. First she'd realize all her loved ones were dead, and then she'd come to the understanding that everything she experienced in the past, everything she planned for the future, was now irrelevant.

Beth held the toddlers as if they were her own grandchildren. "There, there. Shhh, Tara. Hug Ninny. That's a good girl."

Now the only sound was crying.

We'd found somebody to be with, but they needed us as much as we needed them.

We sat there until Sarah gained her composure. She stood up and we all walked together. I led the way as if I knew where I was going. I didn't, but faked it.

We made our way to the second overpass Beth and I had climbed earlier. The only sound was that of footsteps. The smell of dirty diapers filled the air, but was a break from all the other smells we had become accustomed to, almost refreshing. The children were all sleeping. They had all played themselves out from crying. Now was a good time to rest. I was exhausted. Water was our first priority, but this fever had me drained.

Our little party of refugees took shelter underneath that overpass. Water would have to wait until we woke up.

With so much on my mind, sleep evaded me. Maria and I were still awake, the rest were out. I listened to Maria praying. She didn't realize that I was awake too. Beth must surely have been sleeping, or she would have made a comment. Maria hadn't talked since we met. This was the first time I'd heard her voice.

Chapter 14
Awakened by the Breakdown of Society

I didn't sleep much. I was continually getting up to go to the bathroom. Let me rephrase that. I kept getting up to walk about fifty feet away from everybody, to spill myself someplace, away from where we would be walking.

The cloth that I had stored just for this purpose had run out. Both sleeves of my shirt had to be sacrificed. I couldn't wait until this thing was over, maybe it would dehydrate me enough to kill me.

No. I had convinced Beth to keep going because of the firemen's sacrifice. Something called beaver fever was not going to kill me; I wouldn't let it. We'd go back to Mick and get some more water and make a plan so that everybody would win. I could talk to Mick. Once everybody else learned that we now had two other nurses with us, they should accept us. I wondered if they would accept the children. I really needed to find or make a weapon. I was worried about the tower being so valuable.

After my fifth or sixth trip to the privacy of the darkness, I made my way back to the underpass. Just before I reached home, I heard five gunshots ring out in the area of the Dome. They sounded like they all came from the same gun, just as fast as you could pull the trigger. I'm not an expert, but they sounded like shots from a smaller caliber pistol, like a thirty-eight caliber, or something similar. It wasn't as big as a forty-four caliber. A friend of mine used one when we went hunting together. With most of the buildings gone, sound traveled further than it did when all the sounds of the city drowned them out, so it was hard to be sure.

Even though I couldn't see, I ran towards the survivors from the hospital, and Beth. When I got to where they could be seen, I noticed Beth had already taken control of the situation. The babies were being gently muffled while they were crying. Each nurse had one or two children in their arms and were either holding them tight, reassuring them or muffling them.

"Shh, baby shh. Quiet honey, shh" were the only sounds after the shots were fired.

"What's going on?" I asked Beth. Everyone else was busy with a child.

"Didn't you hear it? Somebody shot down towards the dome." She was back to whispering again.

"Do you think that was the police?" I knew that was a stupid question when I asked it.

Before she could humiliate me, more gunshots rang out in the distance. Then more, only this time some came from the hospital. "Let's take these kids, get some more water, and get away from the city. I've got some ideas."

I was the only man along with three women, and four children. I wasn't about to walk up to the tower with any woman. Rape is one of the evils to show its face when society starts to break down, looting comes first; we'd done lots of that already.

"Why don't we just get to fuck out of here?" Sarah screamed, without thinking about what we would need to do just that.

"We need water." I was going to have to go alone. "I'm not letting any of you go to that tower. You said they were raping and killing already." I looked in the direction of Sarah and Maria. I couldn't help but wonder whether either of them had been raped. "I need some kind of weapon. Everyone keep a lookout for some kind of long pipe, or something sharp, or something I can use as a club." I used to be a bow hunter, but I was sure there would be no bows left functional in the debris. Unless a person had a gun in his pocket, there would be no way to find functional firearms or ammunition.

"I'm not going to let you go up there alone, Nick. You're not going to leave me alone with these kids."

"Those kids are not alone as long as you're with them. They need you. I need you... to keep all the kids quiet and off in the distance. Nobody was there two days ago, nobody will be there now." All the time I was looking on the ground for something I could use as a club or a spear.

"You sneak up on them, like you used to with me. Only this time, do it better. After the first time, I could hear you and... I knew what to expect." Her voice trembled.

I held her close. "Well then how come you never stopped me?"

"Maybe, I wanted to be caught by surprise." She said with tears on her face.

I could taste them.

Chapter 15
Back to the Tower

I found a pipe that was once the water line of a house. Beth and I pulled and twisted until it broke free. Galvanized pipe breaks easily at the elbows. It was about six feet long and worked well as a walking stick too. I guess if it were made of wood, it would have been called a staff.

I had to choose between the small axe and the knife as a backup weapon. The axe would be useful to Beth and the others should I not come back; plus I could keep the knife on my belt loop freeing up my other hand. If I needed it, I could just tear it off, loop and all. With that and my trusty staff in hand, I feared nothing. My real plan was that nobody would be there.

The women and the children were out of hearing distance, or at least they had all the children quiet. Either way, they weren't attracting any attention.

I had to put all my efforts into getting as much water as I could carry, then get away before anybody else got there. I had all the baby bottles and empty soda bottles I could carry in my pack, and the canteens. I decided to toss the soup cans.

I knew I was heading in the right direction. The grade of the land gradually increased. I didn't see any light coming from the tower, no fires, torchlight, or flashlight. That helped me with my pace, since I didn't think I had to sneak as much as I thought I was going to have to. If anybody was there they would have some kind of light.

I had one, and I was practicing all the way up the street with my secret weapon, like some "Cowboy Quick draw."

In the darkness, I could make out the tower and the steel that was piled beneath. Nothing had changed as far as I could tell. Just in case, I started to drag my staff with my right arm behind me, with the broken kinked end of the pipe wedged into my shoulder blade. I started to limp up to the tower house, or what was left of it. I felt that anybody seeing a limping man would underestimate him and lay off of their attack.

Nothing made me suspicious and I almost felt it was safe, when I heard some metal roofing move.

"Do you want to get supper, or do you want to be supper?" A voice in the black yelled out.

My heart went into high gear. "I just want some water and I'll leave you alone. Can you spare some? My cats are still thirsty, and all I want to do is... is wash my hair. I'll trade you two cats for the water." Once I spotted a second man, I was sure it was a good idea to have them underestimate me and think I was a senile old man.

I slowly walked closer to them, dragging my staff behind me.

"Stop right there, motherfucker. You want some water, you are going to have to pay for it."

I couldn't see who was talking to me in the dark. They were hiding behind some steel that had been thrown to the side.

"My cats, I just want to get some water for my cats, I have some tuna fish cans here. Here pussy, pussy, pussy." Little did they know that I was talking to them and not my imaginary cats. My former state of weakness was replaced with a cocky fearlessness; adrenaline was pushing me into a confrontation. Their shadows appeared behind sheets of distractingly noisy steel. Apparently my disguise had fooled them. They were leaving the security of the darkness to confront the poor crippled crazy person they had expected might taste good with creamed corn.

When I felt there was enough room to confront both of them at the same time, I stopped. I kept quiet while waiting for them to creep out of the shadows like demons out of a nightmare. I couldn't make out their faces, but I knew what they had in mind.

I jiggled my left arm to adjust the location of the flashlight, like a magician would do with trick flowers. I felt as I had when bow hunting in upstate New York. There were times when I was the predator and deer were the prey. I felt like the predator once again. I was just biding my time for the strike. I knew what I had to do to save us all.

These guys were scum and wouldn't be missed, and really shouldn't be allowed to be involved in creating the next generation of men. Man didn't need their DNA in the gene pool.

I let them both get closer to me. My staff was about six feet long. I figured I could let them get at least eight feet away and then strike.

"Looks like he'd be pretty tuff, don't he?" the skinny one said. I recognized the bogus southern accent.

"Tuff like he might kick our asses, or tough like we might have to chew him longer," the bigger one said.

They both laughed the way crazy people did in the movies.

"Keep laughing boys," I said just low enough so they couldn't hear.

"Bring us all your cats, and we'll give you water." They seemed to be stalling, sizing me up. I had to act fast.

"Blow me asshole." I said defiantly hoping to draw a confrontation.

Amazed at the cockiness of a crippled man, they decided to teach me a lesson. "Git that cocksucker," one of them said.

They both charged at me. As soon as they were about ten feet away, I drew my secret weapon. With one swift, well-practiced move, I slid the flashlight down my sleeve and turned it on. I shined it into their eyes. It stopped one of them.

As the light flared, I swung my staff. Because I had it anchored against my shoulder, I could swing it with leverage and power.

It connected with Tex, knocking off his hat. He dropped in his tracks. When it collided with his head, the sound reminded me of a pumpkin when it hits the road at thirty miles an hour. I know. I tossed pumpkins when I was a kid. The impact jarred my hand and I dropped the pipe.

I tried to shine the flashlight in the face of the bigger one, but all it did was to let him know exactly where I was. He bulldogged me onto my back. I landed on some jagged metal, and dropped the light. It rolled over to where Tex was laying. I reached for my knife. His hands were around my throat, and I couldn't breathe. His right leg had my left arm pinned to my side. I could feel my knife but I couldn't move my hand enough to break it free. I was not going to let go of it for anything. My right hand was all I had to protect myself with.

I wasn't just fighting to save my own life, but to save the life of those four children and their nurses. One of them was Beth.

I reached up with my right hand and dug my finger into the eye of this big bastard who was trying to kill me. My finger went into the orbital socket as eye goo ran down my arm. He still didn't let go. I clawed, punched, and dug at him as fiercely as I could. A tidal wave of fear overcame me. Not the fear of dying, but the realization that I had failed the others. I started to black out when he just went limp and fell on top of me. When he fell, he released his death grip on my neck. I could feel warmth all around him. He was all covered in blood and so was I. Close to passing out from lack of oxygen, I still had enough consciousness left to be confused by the blood. I could smell it. Other than his eye, I had done little damage.

It took a few attempts to roll his limp corpse off my chest. I saw Beth, shaking, vomiting and crying all at the same time. She had the Leatherman in her hand.

She had killed the big guy before he killed me. Being a nurse she knew just where to stab a man for the quickest, most efficient kill. She had stuck him under his arm and lacerated an artery, then again in his chest under his arm, piercing his lung. One last jab in his mid back sliced his liver.

She never had time to reach his carotid artery. He collapsed before she could.

"Nick, Nick, I'm sorry I followed you, but I couldn't let you leave us alone." She bent down to pick up the flashlight that was still on.

I tried to talk but my windpipe was crushed and I was worrying about breathing, let alone talking. Air was getting in, but only enough to make me crave more.

"Breathe, Nick, breathe." She shined the light into my eyes. "You'll be fine in a couple of minutes." After diagnosing me, she kept on to the business that I was unable to do.

As I recuperated I was amazed at how quickly she left me to fill the containers.

Beth twisted the pipe wrench and filled the canteens, baby bottles and soda bottles. "You still okay over there?" she asked as she worked, her voice uneasy.

"Mm hmm," was all I could muster at the time.

She set the flashlight down on waist-level pipes. I could see her for the first time in a long time. Still crying, and shaking, she stripped, and washed the blood off with the lukewarm water from the leaking pipe. Then she turned the flashlight towards me. "Are you feeling better?"

I slowly got to my feet and stripped down. I was covered in blood and shit. I didn't answer her.

After washing myself and my clothes, I put the same wet clothes back on. I had thought about taking the clothes off the two dead guys, but one was covered in as much blood as I was. We did take Tex's clothes. We could use the material for torches, or toilet paper.

Beth carried the backpack as we started back to the others, leaving the two bodies where we had laid them. When I panned the area to see where I was going, the flashlight caught something. I went back to it to see what it was. There on a pole was a human head. Upon closer inspection I could tell it was Mick's. His nametag was pinned to his face. He had been too free with information. Too many people wanted the type of escape that he kept in his pocket. He'd said it was like money now.

"I bet they have his retirement fund. I bet it's still in the tower."

"We'll look for it, but if we find it, then I'm in charge of it and you don't tell anybody about it. Okay?" she said.

"No way. Look what happens when you talk too much." I pointed to Mick's head.

We walked back up to the tower and looked on the bodies and all around, but no drugs could be found. Mick must have taken their location to his grave—as if he was given one.

I double-checked each man's pockets. "I was hoping these guys might have a gun or some kind of a weapon. They didn't even have so much as a knife or a pipe like I did. I don't think they had been here long. They weren't well organized or anything. I wonder if they were even the ones who killed Mick. It would have been hard to cut off his head without a knife."

"I think they were guarding this place for somebody else. These guys didn't seem like they had the initiative to do this on their own. They were probably put here to frighten people away. Whoever put them here probably didn't expect them to encounter anyone anyways." Beth paused. "Let's get to hell out of here. Whoever's eating Mick's body is going to need a drink soon. I don't want to be here when they do."

Chapter 16
One More

We walked in the dark, not wanting to waste the batteries in the flashlight.

It was hard to walk because we drank as much water as our bellies could hold while we were at the tower. We were bloated and uncomfortable, but we needed as much water as possible.

"Do you know where we're going now?" she asked.

I hadn't made any long-term plans. "Down to the others, then..." I stopped because I didn't have an answer.

"I'll tell you where we're going, back the way we came. Then to Buffalo. The Eco-Meat plant is on the way. There must be something left. I can get water. You start me a fire when we stop to rest. All those cans of food are still at the building we spent the night in, and I bet that we can find more. There are fewer people in the country, less competition. We need to get away before the diseases start. We need to get the children out. We can't keep them quiet. They're going to attract attention."

"I couldn't agree more." The most important thing of all was she expected me to build a fire. I couldn't let her down. How in the hell was I going to start a fire, short of rubbing two sticks together? I was starting to panic. We were almost with the rest of the group and I hadn't thought of a way to start a fire. *Think, think, think, asshole. Okay. I'll need a strong stick to use as a dowel, then another one to use to hold the top and another one at the bottom, I can use my shoe laces as the string to spin the dowel, I can whittle some dry wood for kindling... Yea that's the ticket, maybe I can; or maybe I can find a battery, some plastic, birch bark, ...* Then I realized that everything I could think of was probably burned already. *Why did she give me the hard part?*

My deep thought was interrupted by the sound of something moving near a dumpster. I immediately went on full alert and reached for my knife. "Hey, get out of here!" I yelled more out of terror than aggression. My tubing was getting cleaned out today.

Whatever it was came running out of the darkness before Beth could turn on the flashlight. Beth found the switch about same time that we both figured what it was.

"I know youse guys," said a small voice with no face.

Beth shined the light on him. I couldn't remember his name, but I recognized the burns on his head and back.

"Marcos, is that you?" Beth pointed the beam directly at his face.

"How do you like your canteens?" he asked. The innocence of his youth spilled out of his smile and all over his cheeks. After all he'd been through, he could still smile.

Beth knelt down in front the boy. "Are you okay Marcos?"

"Can I stay with you? I'm scared and I'm thirsty and I'm hungry. C'mon let's go hide."

"What happened Marcos? What happened to Mick? Where's everyone else?"

"I think there all dead," he said.

"What did you see?"

"Some guys came up behind Irene and cut her neck with a knife. There was more too. I ran away and hid behind a burned bus. I watched where they couldn't see me. I saw the train man fighting with two guys. He was winning for a while, but then the guy who killed Irene helped the other two. He couldn't beat up all three. He started to scream. That's when I ran away."

Beth stood up and examined his wounds. "You can stay with us. There are some more kids you can play with just up the road. We're going to take a long walk and get out of the city. Have you ever been to the country, Marcos?" Beth reached for his hand but he cried out in pain when his arm lifted. His burns were making his skin tighten up to the point that he didn't want to move his arms.

Fortunately Beth was only four foot, eleven and one half of an inch tall. She only had to slouch down a little to hold his hand.

Before she shut off the flashlight, I noticed her gradually stand more upright. She wasn't being lazy. She was doing it to exercise Marcos' arm, to keep it flexible, so he didn't lose his range of motion.

"I think it's starting to rain, I just felt a sprinkle," she said to Marcos.

I went back to thinking about how I was going to build a fire. Now I had to do it in the rain.

We could hear the babies crying. They were in an alleyway between two masonry buildings that hadn't collapsed—actually pretty smart of Beth to put them there. Their crying could only be heard in about one general direction, and it was quickly apparent that it wasn't going to end soon.

Huddled in the far corner the two women held the children, but keeping them quiet proved to be an impossibility.

While Beth gave everyone water, I kept looking for something to build a fire. I walked by Maria. Every now and then the flashlight would cross her face. I could see she had witnessed horrors in the darkness. Even though she was taking care of the little ones, her stare was off into the emptiness, aimed at some imaginary target.

She jumped as if startled. "Does anybody have any cigarettes?" she said without breathing enough air to finish the sentence. The word "cigarettes" was barely audible.

"Do you have a lighter?" I asked.

Without answering she dug into a pocket. Split seconds later she produced a Bic lighter, just like she had so many times on her way out to the designated smoking area,

"Sorry I don't have any cigarettes, but if I could borrow that lighter, I would appreciate it."

She handed it to me without question, put her hands to her face and started crying.

I took off the cross, knelt down and handed it to Maria.

She took both my hands in hers, looked me straight in the eyes and said, "God bless you." Raising my hands to her mouth, she kissed the cross before placing it around her neck.

Chapter 17
Marcos's Inheritance

We headed out of the city. The rain was coming down quite steadily now. It felt great, unusually large drops of lukewarm rain, warmer than any hot summer cloudburst I had experienced. The grime of the city was washing off, but only on the outside, the filth on the inside would always be there. The memories of death, rape and murder would always cloud happy memories of a past that only seemed a dream now.

I looked up into the sky to let the water wash my face. The drops stung and made me blink. When I could keep an eye open long enough, I made out the outline of clouds in between the drops that slammed into my eyeball. Holding my hand up only concentrated the amount of water obscuring vision.

Now that it was raining, building a fire to boil water wasn't needed. Now we had to find a way to catch water. Pots were easy to find since they were in every household. With a small amount of tugging, we freed a large sheet of steel roofing. There was little wood remaining under the bent metal.

We still had water, but decided to fill the canteens and containers while it was raining.

We took all the screws out of the corrugated roofing except one. The one on the corner would be used to hold the two corners together, making a funnel shape. Then we cleaned both sides with cloth. Not like cleaning with an antibacterial soap, but at least it took off most of the soot. Using a few cinderblocks we stabilized our makeshift aqueduct so the saucepot was at the lowest point.

Everyone huddled down on the driest side of a concrete wall that withstood the earthquake. Everyone but Marcos and me. We were the new water gatherers. We stood out in the open where we could capture only the cleanest rain, void of soot and ash.

I could tell the rain felt good on Marcos, he was moving more and crying less.

I felt uncomfortable standing there silent; I never held a good rapport with kids. "How old are you Marcos?" I asked in an attempt to stymie the awkwardness.

"I just turned eleven. Boy, it sure is raining now isn't it, mister?"

We'd never been formally introduced. "My name's Nick. Your shoulders are feeling better aren't they?" The rain must have softened up his sores.

"Mick... just like the man with all the pills? He was nice and the medicine he gave me makes me feel better. He gave me a whole bunch. He told me to only take half of one when it starts to hurt. I still have two bags full."

Now I was actually listening to him. "My name is Nick, with an N. Did you say Mick gave you bags of pills? Do you still have them? Can I see them?"

"He told me never to show them to anyone or even talk about them. I guess he can't get into any trouble now, can he?" He reached into his back pockets and pulled out two baggies, each packed to the point of ripping. He handed them to me. "Don't tell anybody. Mick told me not to."

I thought about what to say for a couple of seconds. "I think we should show these to the nurses, they know more about this stuff than I do. You hold on to it until we get someplace dry. You've got better pockets. Keep it in the baggies, and I'll let you tell Beth. We'll see what she says."

"Okay, Nick." He tucked the overstuffed baggies back into his pockets, being careful not to rip the plastic.

It didn't take long to see that we hadn't washed the steel enough. There was still a lot of soot on the water when we looked at it with the flashlight. We dumped out the water that was in the pot, and proceeded to scrub the roofing again. This time it would be clean enough to drink.

Marcos and I set up the rain catcher again. It was raining so hard that we would accumulate more than we needed in no time.

While we were waiting for the pot to fill up, Marcos and I pulled some more metal off the rubble. We constructed a lean-to to keep the rain off the little ones.

Soon all the bellies were full of water, as were the vessels we carried. The rain was letting up; it was time to move on.

All the time we gathered our gear together, I waited for Marcos to talk to Beth.

She was busy with all the children and didn't respond to anybody who wasn't crying.

Once we started walking, the little ones went to sleep again. We all took turns carrying the babies. Their tummies were full, even if it was only water.

We needed to find food and shelter. I knew that the building where Beth and I had spent the night wasn't much further up the road.

We had trouble finding the structure in the darkness. It stopped raining. I was glad Marcos and I had collected water when we had.

We came to the abandoned car with the doors open. I remembered this one. "We've got to turn around and go back," I said. "I missed the spot that we're going to camp for the night, it's back this way about a mile or so."

"God damn it, I can't carry these kids forever." Sarah was carrying Adam in her right arm, and Eve in her left. She bounced the boy on her hip to adjust the weight. "How in hell can you tell where to fuck we are?"

The abrupt movement woke the child, who started crying immediately. I was appreciative for the interruption because I had never told Beth about the man and the girls, and didn't want to explain how I knew where I was, but especially didn't want them to see the dead priest. We turned back the way we came from one more time.

The wailing was contagious and it wasn't long before all the children were crying, all except Marcos. The crying was intolerable. Marcos and I walked up ahead of the others just to escape the irritation. Beth stayed back with the other nurses and children. I could hear them talking but couldn't hear what they were saying.

"I think you better tell my wife about your pills in your pocket, they could help keep the kids quiet."

"Mick said not to tell anyone about 'em."

"Mick's ..." I couldn't think of anything else to say. I was so inept when dealing with a child. I couldn't tell him that I saw Mick's head on a pole. "Mick's not here is he? Tell her soon, okay?"

"Okay, Nick. I'll tell her."

I half expected him to go running up to Beth. I had a way of driving kids away. It's not that I didn't like them, but they didn't like me. I guess I caught a case of, "Grumpy old man syndrome" before it was due; kind of like some guys having male pattern baldness when they're in their twenties. Often I'd envisioned myself hoarsely screaming at neighborhood boys. "Hey, get away from my apple trees!" I'd yell as I shook my cane.

We walked silently, except for the constant crying. The visions of the man and his daughters in their final resting place appeared in my mind's eye. The more I tried to erase it, the more I thought about it.

I was glad to see the wires that were leading to and from the substation. I knew we were close. I should have noticed them before. This navigation mistake, which was totally my fault, wasted energy—energy that we couldn't afford.

Finally, with the help of the flashlight, the protective fencing appeared. All the women and children went into the block building.

Marcos and I went looking for wood. There was nothing small to be found. We still had the hatchet, and even though there was little kindling, it didn't take long to shave off enough charred bark to get at the dry wood underneath. Marcos made a bundle that was easily carried by wrapping wire around the chips and slivers that I hacked off. The whole thing ended up looking like a ball of copper yarn with the occasional piece of wood sticking out. It would take a pretty big cat whacked out on catnip to play with this yarn.

Looking at the bundle, I came up with an idea for a new torch. But first we had to get the fire going.

"When we get back, you tell my wife what you have in your pocket. Is that understood Marcos?"

"Okay." He continued to gather wood as if I hadn't even spoken.

"Marcos, I'm not kidding." Maybe that was why I wasn't good with kids. I wasn't very patient.

We walked the short distance back to the substation. It was quiet until we walked into the building. A baby's crying broke the silence. The children were being fed food from the wagons we'd left behind; they remained untouched.

"Beth, Marcos has something to tell you." I could tell she wasn't in the mood for games and this had better be important. The relentless bawling was more than she was accustomed to. Her grandchildren had never given her this much torment, but then they always had full stomachs and clean diapers.

Even with all the stress caused by the children, she managed to talk to him with a polite tone in a caring manner. "What do you have to tell me, Marcos? Come over here and tell me what's wrong."

"He told me not to tell anybody," he whispered.

The flashlight pointed directly in my eyes. "It's okay. She's a nurse and she'll know what's right.

After some silent hesitation he eventually built up the courage and walked over to her. "Promise you won't tell anyone?"

"Tell anyone what, Marcos?" Beth asked.

"Don't tell anyone that I showed you these." He struggled to pull the bags of pills out of his overstuffed pockets. One of the bags tore open, revealing its contents on the floor of the building. "Promise you won't tell?"

"Let's see what you've got there." She leaned forward to pick up some of the pills to examine. "Can I borrow your flashlight? I promise I won't tell."

He handed the light to her.

"Thank you."

Now all the nurses' attentions were drawn away from their little patients, though the crying continued. The flashlight was passed around so each could give her own opinion.

"This is Oxycotin," Maria said.

"No it isn't, it's Hydrocodone," Sarah said.

"He's got both." Each hand held a sandwich bag full. "Marcos, Mick gave you these?"

"He said that he would rather have me have them, than have some weasel get them. Do weasels eat them? What's a weasel?"

"Nick, give me your knife. I want to shave a little off one to give to Adam and Megan." They were the children doing most of the crying. Adam had burns on his legs, and Megan cried constantly as if in pain, but showed no obvious wounds.

I reached for my knife only to discover the loop had broken. Two pats of each pocket were enough to tell me that I had lost the most important item we had recovered since we crawled out of that culvert. "I lost my knife, do you still have your tool, you used to kill...ah...stab...uh, or...save me?" I knew that the last thing she wanted was for the other women to know about the tower incident. I also knew she'd never talk about it again.

Beth's right jean pocket still held the tool. She pulled out the murder weapon, opened the blade, and washed it off with water from her canteen.

Gingerly, she shaved off some of the pill. "Here... give this to them, just put it under their tongue." She passed the sliver to Sarah.

Sarah lashed out. "We know how. Remember we were nurses too; in the city... not some retarded country clinic."

"You're a nurse and you still use that word!" From the day Sally was born Beth detested when somebody used the "R" word in a derogatory fashion. "I would think you would be more educated and professional than that, working in the big city and all."

"Just give me some of that," Sarah said as she took some of the shavings and administered them to her tiny patient.

Once the medicine kicked in, it was silent again. Some slept; others stared blankly at the fire. Beth and Sarah swapped glares.

Chapter 18
New Wheels

Adam and Eve started our day with cries of pain. Both had sustained second-degree burns on their hands and lower arms. Eve's face and head showed burn marks where embers had landed. Once one of us was awake, we all were. After all were fed, we made our way towards I-90. Marcos led the way pulling Megan and Tara in one of the wagons. The other contained the remainder of the food and drinks. We all switched off between carrying a child or pulling the wagon with the food, but Marcos refused to give up his turn. He was having too much fun. His burns no longer bothered him. The exercise loosened his tight skin giving him a wider range of motion than simply walking.

It was nice to hear the little ones laughing. Every time the wagon dropped off the tarmac, both Megan and Tara would giggle hysterically. The laughter was contagious. Nobody can avoid laughing when children are enjoying themselves. It took our mind off things for a while

The meat factory was over a mile away. Prevailing westerly winds carried clues to the condition of any food that might have made it through the fire. A ditch running along the road teamed with rats going in both directions. Those coming from the site were noticeably fatter than those heading in the opposite direction. Their squeaks could be heard over the sound of the wagons. I dealt with rats on a daily basis before this happened, but had never seen anything like this. At times they would climb over each other where the ditch narrowed.

"You know we could eat a lot of meat if you let me catch a few dozen of those," I said, already knowing the answer I would get.

"There isn't any fucking way I'm going to eat those filthy things." Sarah's hands waved back and forth. "I'll die of starvation first."

"We might not have any choice," Beth snapped. "There is not going to be any help. We are on our own. There may not be much else to eat for a long time."

Sarah stood silent for at least a minute and then said, "How many would you need to catch to feed all eight of us?"

Step by step, the light of the torch revealed a quarter of the massive structure still stood on the thirty-acre lot. Shells of employee vehicles littered the parking lot. Few bodies were found in or around the parts of the building that had collapsed, though the plant employed hundreds. Thousands of vats used to grow meat could be seen under the twisted steel. Bloated slabs of animal tissue spilled over the edges and onto the floor, only to be gorged on by vermin. The slime oozing along the ground was as slippery as it was putrid. Turning each corner sent the small animals running in all directions. Each time the wind changed, we would be forced to back off and head upwind.

The further we made it into the building, the less fire damage we found; some rooms were untouched. We entered a steel door leading to a stairwell that led us to a parking garage. No longer used for parking, it had been converted to office space, locker rooms, and a mechanic's shop. Rows of lockers containing uniforms lined the walls of showers. That's where I found most of the employees.

I turned around to stop Marcos. I shined the light between us. "Marcos, stay right here while I look around. Don't move from this spot, okay? I will keep talking to you." I didn't want to leave him alone in the dark, but I couldn't let him see what I'd found. "You okay out there?"

"Yes, but it is dark."

I pointed the flashlight at the entrance to the showers. The blue ceramic tile reflected enough light to figure out what happened here. "Is that better?"

"Okay. Can I come in with you now?" His voice echoed.

I could hear him scuff the floor as he started in. "No! You stay out there. I'll be right out." I turned the flashlight back into the showers one more time. About thirty bodies lay in a pool of water inside the shower. No water flowed out of the showerheads, though all the cold handles were turned on high. These people tried to escape the heat by staying under the cold running water. None had burns. The oxygen was sucked outside to feed the inferno. They all died of asphyxiation. "Here I come, Marcos. Let's go back into the mechanic's shop and see if we can find some tools or something." As I turned I caught him looking in.

Together we walked past three more shower stalls, all full.

Inside the workshop we found several large toolboxes containing any tool imaginable. We also found two vending machines. One blow from the back side of our universal key—our ax—unleashed candy bars that no longer held their original shape but were still edible, potato chips of several flavors, corn chips, nuts, meat sticks and jerky. The preservatives had done their job. I loaded up the backpack to bring the treats to the others. Meanwhile Marcos poked around the shop.

"Hey, Nick. Come look at this."

"You be careful over there. What did you find?"

"I don't know. It's some kind of machine with wheels."

I walked over to him. A blue tarp hid whatever it was he found. I pulled the tarp aside to reveal three fork trucks. These old diesel lifts were abandoned for the newer hydrogen cell trucks. Each one still contained fuel and keys. The batteries were all dead, so starting one was impossible. The nearest thing to batteries was the ones used to operate portable drills. A workbench held a drill and three batteries.

"Marcos, hold the flashlight for me." I lifted the seat of one of the older machines to view the engine. The alternator was easily accessible and the tools made disconnecting it a ten-minute job. With the battery removed and on the workbench, I hooked the drill to the alternator and the alternator to the battery. I placed the drill on the shaft of the alternator and turned it on. After about ten minutes the first drill battery went dead and was replaced with another. All three were used until all were dead. I took out the battery of the newest lift and replaced it with the one we'd charged. "Here goes nothing." I turned the key. The battery took a charge, but still had little power. I cranked the engine over and over again, furiously pumping the accelerator for all it was worth. "Come on, baby, come on." The flapper on the exhaust bounced as the engine tried to come to life. Then I noticed the button for the glow plug. I stopped turning the key to activate the glow plug. After waiting a minute I tried the key again. The engine turned over three times, then smoke started coming out of the stack. I didn't stop trying till the engine came alive with a clattering. On came the lights. I let go of the key and it kept running. "Wooo hooo! We ain't walking anymore, Buddy. Wait until the girls see this."

Chapter 19
Junk Food and Smokes

Marcos and I moved as much in the shop as we could by hand, and then used the high lift to move the rest, making a path to the roll door. With no power to raise it, I simply drove the forks through the thin metal, and hit the up lever. Parts from the door opener bounced off the roof of the cab. Dust and ash blew in and made a swirling cloud in front of the light's beam. When the door was high enough, we backed up, lowered our forks, and entered the underground parking lot converted for storage. Rows and rows of metal vats filled the concrete bunker where automobiles once parked. Stacked three high, the shiny stainless-steel coffins were the vats used to grow meat. Apparently the plant had been planning on expanding their herd.

Only a narrow path led the way to the exit ramp. Exhaust bellowed from the ancient workhorse. Black and toxic, the smoke hit the concrete ceiling and curled back down choking Marcos and me.

"Whoa, this thing stinks." Marcos bounced on my knee each time the solid tires of the machine hit a crack in the floor. There were many. The earthquake had lifted the floor two inches in some places. The lights showed one area where the roof had collapsed crushing the vats underneath. The light also showed another thing: the vats were all on wheels. These were not for an expansion. They were a discontinued design. These old vats had been used before the automated line made them obsolete.

I stopped the truck and applied the parking brake, once I found it. "You're going to have to get out. I want to look at something." I left the truck running. "Don't touch anything and stand here."

We walked over to the stack of vats. Marcos wouldn't leave my side. Designed to stack one upon the other, only the bottom one showed its wheels. I could only assume they all had wheels. A coupling device on each told me they could be pulled along in a train.

Upon checking the fork truck it was discovered to have the hookup needed. "Let's go show the others what we found. We can come back later and look around." We climbed back in the cab and headed outside.

It was nice to see the outside light up again. No sooner did we get on level ground than we saw the rest of our group coming to see what the racket was. I put the truck in neutral and let them walk up to us.

"What did you find?" Beth asked.

"How in hell are we all going to ride on that?" Sarah asked.

"We had to make one out of three, but it runs." I pushed down on the accelerator to put more charge in the battery. The light brightened. The exhaust surrounding the group covered the smell of rotting flesh and was welcome with each gust of southern winds.

"There are some vats with wheels we can tow behind. Plus there is a lot of other stuff we can use inside." I threw my backpack down at their feet. "Here is some food we found inside too." When the pack hit the ground, three bags of chips fell out. Tara ran over and picked up her share first before anybody else could react. Beth opened a bag for each child and the crunching began. Marcos and I had dibs on the jerky. We ate in bright light for the first time since this started. We had a picnic in front of the fork truck, though we had no blanket or watermelon. Normally Beth wouldn't let children gorge on candy-machine junk food, but a treat would lift everyone's spirits.

Maria attempted to open a bag of chips for Adam, but it ripped and spilled all over the ground. She put her hands to her face and began to cry. Adam just picked the nachos off the ground one by one and put them in his mouth.

"Why don't you try to eat something?" Beth said while feeding Tara some peanuts. "We've all got to keep up our strength."

"I'm not hungry. Leave it for the kids." Maria continued to cry.

"I know what you might want." I went over and took her by the hand. "Bring the flashlight. There might be a few cigarettes inside." I turned to the others. "I'll bring back some more snacks. Leave the truck running so the battery charges."

I led Maria into the parking garage and down the path to the showers. The first shower stall still held water so we looked in the second. One by one we checked the bodies for a pack of smokes. Half a pack of unfiltered cigarettes were found on a large man after rolling his body over. "Are these the type you smoke?"

"I don't care what kind they are right now." She took one out of the pack. "Do you still have my lighter?"

I didn't want to waste the lighter's fluid, but I thought Maria would appreciate it right then. I handed it to her.

She lit one, took a long drag, and held her head back savoring the smoke. Upon exhaling she coughed uncontrollably. Prepared for the harshness, she took another puff. The red glow at the tip bounced up and down as she shook. One more pull and her shaking lessened. "Are you a man of faith, Nick?" she asked while blowing out smoke.

"What?"

"Do you believe in God?" she asked. The ember glowed brighter.

"Yes, but I haven't been practicing. Why do you ask?"

"Nick, have you ever read the book of Revelation?" A second cigarette was lit off the first. "John wrote of the tribulation. Do you think that's what is happening?"

"I never actually read the whole Bible, just pieces of it."

She coughed again. "I think this might be God's wrath on man, but one thing doesn't make sense." She took another long drag. Again the burning tobacco could be seen shaking. "Why wasn't I drawn up in the rapture? I accepted Jesus when I was a little girl. I've always done his work. I go to church three times a week. If this is the tribulation, then the rapture has already happened. Why am I still here? I should be beside God, not stealing cigarettes off some dead guy. All the signs were there: the earthquakes, the wars. I should have seen it coming. I must have done something wrong to upset God." She needed more time alone with her habit.

I wasn't up on the Bible like Maria, and felt a little uncomfortable. "I'm going to bring some more snacks out to the others. I'll leave you the flashlight. I'll be able to find my way out. You should be able to find a few more packs if you want to look." The running fork truck could be heard outside.

I felt along the concrete wall until the opening could be seen. Seeing the others lifted my spirits. The children played in the beam of artificial light. Marcos made shadow puppets on Sarah's back while Megan and Tara took turns jumping off the forks, which were only three inches off the ground. Each time they fell and rolled, laughing and carrying on like nothing bad had ever happened. "Let's all go in with Maria and see what else we can find. We might be able to find something soft to sleep on for a change." I climbed back on the vehicle. Like a parade, everybody followed me into garage and down the path to Maria.

The headlight lit up her face. The nicotine had worked. "Look, we can change the babies' diapers now." Her hands held several employee uniforms, each with the former wearers name on the pocket. Maria's own pockets bulged with her stash of smokes.

Each child was donned with clean makeshift underwear before any more scavenging was done. With no safety pins, folding became an important skill.

While the others set up camp inside the garage, I tried to hook up the meat vats to the fork truck. The ceiling was too low to unstack the vats where they were placed. Dragging all three outside was the only way to separate them from each other. Each did have their own set of wheels, as I had guessed. Hooked end to end, a train soon materialized.

Knowing it could be done, it was time to shut off the truck and hope it would start again. It had run for about an hour, plenty of time to charge the battery. I shut it off. Crossing my fingers on my left hand while turning the key with my right, the engine restarted. Once again I shut it off to conserve fuel. Where to find more would be the next challenge.

Again I made my way in the dark back to the others. Marcos had led them all into the garage where no bodies laid. This would be our room for the night. Beth made a nest of the uniforms in the cleanest corner for all of us to sleep on. The three little girls had already picked a spot and were sleeping. Marcos and Adam were looking around the room.

Sarah ate some of the snacks herself. "How are we supposed to sleep with this smell?" The bodies in the showers had started to decompose.

A banging sound drew my attention to the two boys. Adam pounded on the side of an oil tank used to fuel a small heater used in the shop. A two hundred seventy-five-gallon tank sat behind some fifty-gallon barrels. I walked over to them. "Let me see your flashlight, Adam." The little guy handed it over and amused himself with a spray can of paint. He shook it to and fro listening to the ball bearing rattling around inside. The tank's gauge read full. Although it held kerosene, it could still be used in the fork truck. One more vat would be needed to transport the tank. Two hundred gallons or more would take us a few hundred miles, but finding more would be difficult.

Twenty-two full water jugs stood next to fifteen empty ones. Three more flashlights were found in the showers with the dead. Maria found them while looking for cigarettes.

Once the boys were quieted down, the rest of us picked a spot in the nest. I lay down next to Beth. Together we listened to the little snores coming from the children. To them, today was a long one filled with play. They were exhausted. The only other sound was Maria's praying. Beth elbowed me. I elbowed her back with a little more enthusiasm. I whispered, "Shh, now is not the time." I knew she wanted to say something, and I knew what it might be.

Despite the odor, even Sarah did her share of the snoring.

Chapter 20
The Hay Ride

I woke with light in my eyes, not daylight, but Adam shining the flashlight right in my face. The air seemed to have cooled down, enough so we all crept closer to each other in our sleep. Maria still slept, with Megan curled up next to her. Beth and Tara huddled together, and Sarah snuggled with Eve. Marcos slept alone. I'm not sure whom Adam had slept with. He appeared to be the early bird amongst the group. Once he noticed I was awake, he turned the light on Marcos. But that wasn't enough to cause a stir, so he kicked him. I laughed.

"Hey, stop it." Marcos rolled over and pulled more shirts and pants over his arms and head. He tried to go back to sleep, but Adam continued kicking him. Finally Marcos could take no more. He saw I was awake too and got up.

"Shh." I put my finger to my lips and motioned for him to come over to me. Both the boys stumbled over the uniforms in my direction. "Let's go see what we can find and we'll let the others sleep." I whispered.

Marcos and I left the nest to look around. Adam tripped on the pile of garments landing on Sarah.

"Will you fucking lie down and go to sleep?" Sarah snapped.

I grabbed Adam's hand. "Go back to sleep. I'll keep them quiet. Come on boys, let's go over here. Shh."

She too pulled more clothing over herself and Eve. They both snuggled closer to each other. Eve whined a little, but immediately went back to sleep.

I could guide the boys with the beam of light, the way an equestrian controls a horse in the ring. We made our way to the other side of the garage. A fifty-gallon drum of motor oil held a hand pump. With some minor alterations it could be made to reach the bottom of the fuel tank. The mechanics had a coffee pot on the workbench. Although there was no electricity to run the device, there had to be a can of coffee somewhere in the cupboards. I looked in each and every one, but no foodstuffs of any kind could be found. Each space contained parts and cleaning supplies, but no coffee. It was only when we cut locks from personal lockers that we found the stash of the person who made coffee. Three cans of the stimulant sat in his locker along with two bags of sugar and two jars of creamer. Another can contained a bucket of money, mostly change, and useless in this new world. I wanted to look in more lockers, but Adam kept knocking things over or banging on one thing or another. I tried to keep him quiet so the others could sleep.

"Hey, Nick, look. Can we use this?" Marcos held up a work light. The cord was only about three feet long, but could be adapted to work off the battery of the high lift.

"Yes we can. Give it to me so the bulb doesn't get broken."

"Please and thank you!" Beth said, coming out of nowhere.

"God damn it, Beth. You scared the shit out of me." Then I realized my diarrhea had subsided, and I'd never noticed. "How long have you been standing there?"

"Long enough to know we'll have cheese doodles and coffee for breakfast." She kissed me good morning. "Boy, it got cold didn't it?" A blue uniform hung over her shoulders like a sweater. The nametag said "Smyth." Tara slept with her head on Beth's shoulder. "She reminds me of Sally. She farted all night long," she whispered.

I touched Tara's head, careful not to wake her. "I'll start a fire to make coffee. We'll eat, then get stuff together and head for Buffalo."

"Can we make it all the way with the fuel we have?"

"I doubt it. But we shouldn't have too far to walk when we run out."

Beth shifted Tara over to the other shoulder. "Do you think Buffalo is going to be in any better shape than Syracuse? All the cities are going to be exactly the same."

I snapped the handle of a push broom into three pieces over my knee. "Seen any more brooms?" I asked.

Two brooms and a shovel handle later, the coffee was on.

All the adults surrounded the pot of hot water when the grounds were immersed. Not exactly espresso, but the end result would be the same. The aroma of coffee after so long without it overwhelmed an olfactory system desensitized by the constant smell of death. The perfume from the mountains of Columbia transported us away from reality for a moment. Once again I sat at my kitchen table checking the news online before heading off to kill the neighborhood pest, my third coffee steaming my glasses. I imagined Beth was transported to the dining hall of the hospital. Maria's and Sarah's minds seemed to wander as they too inhaled not only the brewing drink, but the can of grounds as well. The smell alone was enough to change our demeanor. Somehow our day brightened even though it was still dark. Some hidden message in our wiring said this is the way a day was supposed to begin.

The children were fed, the wagons were hitched, and supplies were gathered. We were Buffalo bound. Five stainless steel bathtub-looking things being towed by an ancient work horse, all used to make fake food to feed the masses, was a sight to behold. Two cars could hold passengers. The occupants would rest comfortably on bedding made from several layers of company uniforms. Assorted snacks were at the reach of each guest, though the littlest guests were not allowed to reach them. Each car had its own water supply in the form of plastic water jugs (twenty-three in total). The third car in the train held the whole oil tank, estimated volume: two hundred gallons. Lifting it was no problem considering the engine of the train was a forklift. We filled the fourth vat with wood. Some of the bathroom walls in the garage were sacrificed. The caboose held assorted tools, extra batteries, more uniforms, water, and the fifty-gallon drum of motor oil.

"C'mon everybody, we're going on a hay ride!" Beth set Tara down in the first portable vat.

"No, here!" Tara squealed, then immediately ran over to the other side of the trailer.

Marcos jumped onto the wagon, without asking the "Queen of the wagon's" permission.

Tara ran over and hit him on the back. "Noooooooooooo. Mine!" Then she utilized every centiliter of air in her little lungs to force out a shrill scream that lasted so long she nearly passed out. After "The scream heard around the world," as coined by Sarah, Tara got all quiet. She just stood there quivering with a surprised look on her face. We all broke out in laughter. She started to cry and catch her breath at the same time. It wasn't working. The rapid in and out movement of air through those little vocal cords made a sound that Sarah also described as, "a chipmunk on acid." That made us all laugh louder.

Beth decided it was time to intervene. "Don't you pick on my baby," she said. "C'mon, honey, you come to Ninny. Those meanies. They better leave my baby alone." She picked up Tara and hugged her. The toddler instantly stopped crying and wrapped her legs around Beth's waist. I couldn't see, but I'm sure the old crocodile tears were flowing.

We were ready to travel.

The antique fired up without hesitation. "Is everybody holding on?" I put the lever into the forward position. I could feel the transmission shift through my seat. The clunk of the pin that held the trailer was a sign we had begun to move.

More laughter came from the wagon as we began to roll. It was short lived because the engine's pistons slapped like a metronome and put the little ones to sleep like a recording of white noise.

Traveling along the thruway proved difficult due to cars piled up near underpasses just like the trip down to Syracuse. This time we could use the high lift to move them out of the way, bodies and all. Another thing I wasn't counting on was how badly the trailers whipped side to side the faster we went. To prevent this we could only travel at half throttle. Though it took longer, safety was more important than speed.

While riding, Beth and the others sorted the uniforms. Those that wouldn't fit any of us were cut into diapers, toilet paper cloth, and torch fuel. They also made torches. The specifications I described were followed to the letter.

After spending long hours riding, everyone needed a break. We stopped along an area with water on both sides of the road. If any danger approached us, we would see it coming. I started a fire, and then shut off the truck to check the fuel and oil. After adding both, I walked with the others to stretch my legs.

Marcos sat at a culvert tossing pebbles into the water. I walked over to him while the smaller children were being tended to. "Would you like to drive a while when we get going again?" I asked.

He stopped tossing stones. "Are you serious? Yes. Do you think I can?"

At the speed we were moving, I could intervene if he should get into trouble. "I'll be sitting right beside you."

"If I do good enough, can I drive a car someday?"

"Sure." I didn't have the heart to tell him that even I might never drive a car again.

He picked up a couple more stones. "Think I can hit that animal out there with a rock?"

"What animal?" I looked where he threw last, but nothing could be seen. "Wait a minute, let me listen." A chewing sound could be heard about thirty yards out in the water. I couldn't see anything on top of the surface except thousands of cattail shafts. Only an inch stood above the water line, resembling the stubble on a man after five days without shaving. I shined the light towards the sound just in time to see a muskrat break the surface. "I see it. That's a muskrat. If I could catch a few, we could have fresh meat for supper."

"But Sarah said she wasn't going to eat rats." Marcos said.

"These are a different kind of rat than what she was talking about. These only eat plants and are very clean. I think she'll eat anything if she gets hungry enough." Figuring how to catch them would take a little thinking. As a nuisance wildlife trapper, I seldom received calls to trap them. They caused little damage and seldom invaded households. When one did get into some old lady's house during the spring breeding season, it was easily shooed out the door with a broom, never to return.

Catching them here required a different tactic. Finding where the aquatic rodents crossed under the road would be crucial to my success. Once the culvert was found, a trap could be designed. "Let's go back to the train. You and I have a lot of work to do." I started jogging back to the others. Soon a race developed.

I had a shadow in the dark, and he was gaining. Now my jog was turning into a full-blown sprint. We were only about fifty yards from the others. The fire showed a clear path down the track. Not one burned vehicle cluttered the road. They'd all driven off into the water when the fires came, choosing a death by drowning over burning, in the same manner jumpers escaped the flames of a burning building.

Only one thing stopped me from beating him back to the others, and that was because Marcos was a fifth my age. I still had a breathless twenty yards left to walk when he skidded to a halt in front of Beth. "Me and Nick are going to catch some rats."

"I said I'm not going to eat those filthy things," Sarah said.

I couldn't hear all Marcos said as he explained the difference between the two rats due to my heavy breathing and pounding heart.

"I don't care what kind of rat they are, they're still rats," Sarah said. "I'm not eating them."

"That's good," I said, still trying to catch my breath. "I'm not sure I can catch very many anyway."

"More for the rest of us," Beth murmured.

Sarah's sneer was highlighted by the flickering light of the fire. The glares and the temperatures were getting colder.

I escaped to the solitude of the wagon train, emptied the drum of motor oil into five of the empty water jugs, and dumped the remainder into the ditch. The environment was fucked at this point. I didn't feel any guilt.

Using a screwdriver and hammer from the toolbox, I slowly and loudly chiseled the cover off the metal drum. The sound echoed and I was sure could be heard for miles. I was concerned the noise might draw unfavorables, yet I continued. First the top, then the bottom was cut out and discarded; chicken wire along the road would funnel the furbearers into the drum where they would drown before escaping. Marcos helped me lower the contraption into the water in front of the culvert. "Four or five hours should be enough time to trap enough rats to give us all a taste of fresh meat," I said, as we walked back to the others.

While I waited for supper to find its way into my fifty-gallon pantry, I swapped batteries out in the fork truck. As long as it was running, I could unhook the charged one and replace it with a dead one. As the vehicle ran, the new battery charged, leaving the charged one to be used as a power source for the drop light.

I needed to rest awhile. I was starving and out of energy. I watched the kids from the ground. Keeping them away from the fire was chore number one. Maria hovered over it ensuring their safety, and tending a pot of boiling water. Filling the empty water jugs with potable water every time we built a fire was the new protocol. Each time the water in the pot would reach a rolling boil for fifteen minutes or so, she would pour it into an empty container and put more filtered swamp water on the fire.

"We're almost out of food," Beth said while changing Tara. "We've only a few cans of tomatoes left."

"Marcos, give me a hand to check if we caught anything yet." We walked to the culvert to pull out the drum. Once we got it up to the road, we found three dead muskrats in our trap. I showed Marcos how to clean them. I tossed the guts and fur into the water.

The pot we had taken from the coffee locker held the boneless meat. After searing it to a golden brown over the fire, I dumped in a can of tomatoes.

"What to hell is that?" Sarah couldn't talk without swearing.

"Salisbury rat." I tried to say it without snickering.

She came over to sniff. "You know that doesn't smell too bad." After going without for so long, her fussiness seemed to be lessening. "Come on everybody. Supper's on."

No leftovers remained in the bottom of the pot. The texture of real meat was as welcome as the aroma. Nobody missed Phony Bologna.

Chapter 21
Dazed and Confused.

Moving automobiles from underneath underpasses used more fuel than I wanted to waste, but it was the only way to continue to Buffalo. Several times the wagons needed to be unhooked to maneuver the fork truck. Many miles had passed from the last blockade and we were rolling smoothly, when we noticed some of the burned vehicles had more damage than others we had seen along the way. I turned the light of the fork truck in the direction of the vehicles. Two cars were flipped on their sides. The skeleton of a semi came into view with only the chassis remaining. Apparently the truck carried some volatile fuel that exploded during the fire. I was so busy looking at the damage, I missed the crater created by the BLEVE (boiling liquid expanding vapor explosion—something I learned when I was in the fire department). Whatever the rig carried created a hole in the blacktop nearly four feet deep.

The fork truck shuddered as it tried to skid to a stop. The trailer's weight pushed it ever closer to the crater. The nose of the truck dropped and momentum abruptly ceased. Everyone in the train lurched forward, some nearly falling out entirely. Some of the supplies tipped over and landed on one of the children.

The sudden stop caused me to slam my head into the windshield. The force of my skull impacting the Plexiglas windshield caused the nearly indestructible material to break in half. I fought unconsciousness by thinking about how much the others depended on me. I needed to stay awake. I grabbed hold of the levers that raise and adjust the forks to avoid falling off entirely. The fork truck stalled out. I couldn't prevent it. Stunned, I sat back down on the seat and struggled to ask if everyone was all right. Before I could muster the ability to speak clearly, I heard a now familiar voice.

"What to fuck are you doing?" Sarah screamed.

All the children were crying. I managed to turn to see the nurses doing their assessments of each patient.

Eve was screaming, while the others were only crying.

"I fell on her when he stopped so quickly," Sarah said, trying to put the blame on anyone but her. "I think her arm might be broken."

I heard other things, but was having a difficult time staying conscious.

The next thing I remember was Beth shaking me. "Nick, Nick... Are you all right?" She shined a flashlight in my face.

"What happened?" I was groggy. I knew Beth was talking, but couldn't clearly understand her.

She was checking my pupils, and though the light was hurting my eyes, I was unable to resist her. She turned my head from right to left looking into each ear.

I was tired and needed a nap. I didn't care about the fork truck, the children or anyone. I just needed a nap. All I remember is Beth helping me to the ground with the sound of a child crying in the distance.

In a state of semi-consciousness, I heard Beth's voice. I remember taking a pill. I remember the sound of Beth and Sarah arguing. My body was powerless. My head ached horribly.

I don't recall how long I lay there on the road.

Beth startled me by shining the light in my eyes again. "Can you get up and climb in?" Somehow they got me to my feet. I rolled into the first vat in the line of five, and that's all I clearly remember.

I thought Beth was checking my eyes again, but realized it was the sun high in the summer sky. This time the light didn't hurt my eyes. I was in my backyard during a barbeque. Sally bounced on my knee, while Beth played with Sally's cousins on the swing set. The wind blew a gentle breeze, but sounded different somehow, like a predictable monotonous mechanical heartbeat.

I lifted the cover of a grill I've never owned. This one looked like a homemade version of a smoker, all stainless steel, with wheels. I placed enough faux frankfurters on the searing hot grate to feed each family for the next three days. Beth would make up take home trays when they all left.

I felt my face's muscles pull back into a smile. Then I turned to my right to see Marcos playing on the swing. Beth never even said a word. I was confused. I'd never met Marcos back home before, or had I?

While I thought about it, I opened up the lid of the grill to turn the dogs. I started to turn about thirty Phony Bologna wieners, when they turned into harry muskrats, tails and all. Their flesh burnt to a crisp.

Surprised, I stepped back to think. Something was wrong, but I couldn't figure out what it was. I looked for Beth to see what her reaction to this was but couldn't find her. Panic ran through my body. I could count my heartbeat without looking for a pulse.

Suddenly I knew we were going up a hill. The fork truck bellowed and I smelled the sooty exhaust. I felt acceleration as we rolled down the other side. I sensed every bump and joint in the pavement. The wheels on the vats were made of solid rubber. The vats were not designed with suspension. Due to the constant joints in the road, I was fading out again.

Again, I was in my backyard. This time it was dark. Sally and the other grandkids were gone. Marcos must have gone home too. The grill cover was red hot, and black smoke billowed from the sides. I met flames when I lifted the cover and stepped back. I felt my eyebrows singe. There in the huge grill, I envisioned Beth charred like the dogs that turned into rats. I reached down to lift her out when some of her flesh tore from her body. As I pulled my burning hands away, the crucifix the priest gave her caught on my finger. As I pulled harder the chain cut into the burnt flesh of her beautiful neck. The more I tried to prevent it, the more it dug in. I screamed.

The fork truck slowed. "Nick, are you okay?" She stopped the rig and came running back to my personal car. "Nick?"

I had never been so glad to see her face as I was at that point. The nightmare was over and I still had her. "My head is killing me. Please give me a kiss."

She did. She was as glad to see life in my eyes as I was to see life in hers. I took another pill and went back to sleep. My perceived reality depended on whether I was awake or not. Both felt eerily real. I faded in and out of dreams from the past, but it was hard to distinguish which one was a nightmare and which one wasn't. I thought we were heading back the way we came. I didn't question why, where, or how we were going; I had all I could do to know that we were.

Chapter 22
Thank God for the Amish

The couplings of the wagons clinked together, telling me we were stopping. Still groggy, I could tell the light of the truck was being moved though the vehicle remained parked. I sat up to see Beth and Sarah walk ahead. I didn't know what they were looking at, but I heard both of them scream. Their shrill squeals were soon followed by intermittent laughter.

"What's going on up there?" I had all I could do to lift my head over the side of the vat. My head felt like it weighed fifty pounds. The light of the forklift hurt my eyes even though it was aimed forward away from me. I felt sleepy again and lay down. They would get me if they needed me.

I lifted the grill one more time to check the dogs. Again the smoke curled around my head. During the summer my eyes were always bloodshot due to the smoke of my grill. My next memory took me to the Yoder farm. Mr. Yoder handed me two steaks and said they had another gift for me.

Mrs. Yoder came out of the house with something in her hands. When she got closer, I noticed the woman was Beth in Amish garb, not Mrs. Yoder. She held something that seemed to squirm in her hands. "Don't touch it. It'll bite your finger off." Again I was confused, but I was getting used to it. I knew she was alive and these were only hallucinations. I could rest in peace. But when the thing in her hands turned into a snapping turtle, I knew this was a concussion-related dream. As she drifted away the turtle turned into the cross and chain the priest had given her. This was all a hallucination that would soon go away.

The train began to move again. The jolt brought me to a consciousness I hadn't experienced in days. "Where are we going?" I asked Maria, who was in the adjoining car.

"We're heading south to Pennsylvania. I told the others there are a lot of Mennonite farms from here and all the way to the bottom of the state. Beth didn't want to go, but then reconsidered. We have seen remnants of Amish farms, but no Mennonites yet.

"Why does it make a difference? None of them would have survived," I said, more awake than I'd been in a long time. My headache had subsided.

"Many of the Mennonites use the old tractors, those that ran on diesel, just like this machine, right? I knew a few of them down in the lower half of New York. More live in Pennsylvania. I suggested we head south because we could find fuel. I hope I didn't do wrong suggesting it to them." Maria lit a cigarette.

The train stopped again. Beth got down. Marcos followed her to the front. This time it was Marcos who carried the shelled reptile. The first one was not a dream. I looked in the vat behind me and saw three animals crawling over each other, two smaller painted turtles and one big snapper. "Thinking about having seafood for supper?" I asked Beth as she went past back to the fork truck.

"I thought we could keep them for when you can't catch us some food," she responded.

Hours passed till the lift needed more fuel. "How much is left?" I asked Beth as she pumped more fuel into an empty water jug.

"It's hard to tell," she said. "Maybe enough to fill up two or three times more. We need to find a place with an old burned tractor with iron wheels.

"Iron wheels, what are you talking about?"

"The Mennonites used tractors, but they weren't allowed to use wheels with rubber. When we find steel wheels, we may find more diesel fuel. We just need to find their underground tank."

She climbed aboard and we were on our way. I lay back down to get more rest. The engine sang its tired song, lulling me to sleep.

I woke when we stopped. I found enough energy to set our barrel trap in another culvert hoping to catch some more muskrats. Marcos wired the drum to the culvert preventing its movement in the current. We had no more food. The children would go hungry for a few more hours. The turtles would be kept for more dire times when nothing could be caught. I built a fire and water was placed on to boil. One by one each child's crying ceased as they went to sleep. No shelter was needed. No precipitation fell, though the air seemed cooler. Little wood could be found in the area. What we did find along the ditches remained underwater and needed to be dried.

After what seemed like three or four hours, Marcos and I checked the inside of the trap. It held three more muskrats. Three seemed to be our lucky number. I skinned them and was about to throw away the guts and the fur when Beth came over to me and asked, "Could we use those furs for anything?"

I washed my hands off in the pond water. "I can't imagine what you would use them for, but I'll put them in the back."

All were fed and we were on our way again. Sprinkles of rain started to fall on the windshield and on our passengers. With no tops over the wagons, the children were getting damp. We needed to find steel roofing. The first home we came to supplied the material needed. I bent the steel to keep the rain off everyone's head, but the vats slowly gathered water at the bottoms. We needed to find shelter.

"Look, there's a metal wagon wheel beside that foundation. These must have been Amish," Maria said.

I shined the light beam over towards the stone cellar. "This was an Amish house, they won't have any fuel for the truck, but their garden should be close by." The growing season was nearing an end, but harvest season had been interrupted by the end of the world. We all took some time to dig through the soil next to where the barn used to stand. Nothing remained above ground, but after some poking around in the rich dirt, small potatoes and turnips showed themselves. Carrots and beets were found in other rows, the withered and burnt plants above ground revealed their locations.

The barn had been shadowed by a silo at one time. The barn had burned to the ground, but the silo remained. The old concrete structure withstood the earthquake that toppled larger buildings in the city. Though no roof covered the vertical cylinder, it was the only shelter for miles. Since the corn missed harvest, it was nearly empty. We decided to camp out in it for supper.

I started a fire in the center with what dry wood we had. The smoke swirled as the wind blew occasional drops of rain in on us. One side of the silo remained nearly dry, so that's where we took cover from the elements.

Soon the pot was stuffed with vegetables. We were full for the first time since this happened. After eating the children were getting restless. They would run around and around the inside of the circular hotel. On the far side, a puddle of water formed the more it rained. Of course each one was drawn to it, splashing each time they went past. Their shoes weren't waterproof. Only Tara refrained from the chase game. Her vice was the fire.

Beth constantly asked Tara to keep away from it, but she was mesmerized by flames. She would toss any remaining boards back into the flames after they had tumbled out.

"C'mon, honey. Get back before you get burned." Beth said for the hundredth time.

Sarah had enough. "Why don't you just crack her on the ass. We're all getting sick of hearing you begging her to get away. Make her. Stop letting her get away with murder." She spoke for all of us, and no one objected.

"Mind your own business. You've got all you can do with Eve. Her feet are soaked." Beth was very defensive when it came to Tara.

"At least I'm not yelling at her all the time. That's what's annoying." Again cold glares were exchanged.

As if on cue Tara picked up one more piece of wood that had fallen back from the embers. This time, it was still glowing on the end she grabbed. She shrieked with pain.

"There, now she'll learn," Sarah said as she quickly reached for some cold water to stop the burning.

Beth was looking at the baby's hand, as Sarah attempted to pour water over the blisters. "I'll do it, just get away from me." She took the water, spilling a quarter of it as she jerked the canteen away.

"Well you got what you wanted, didn't you?" Sarah said to Tara.

I half expected Beth to push her into the fire. "Well let's go and get some more wood Marcos," I said. We were low, plus it was an excuse to get away from the constant bickering. The baby had second-degree burns on her thumb, which Beth tended.

We set up racks to dry shoes, clothes and wood. Steam came from all three, though care had to be taken not to scorch the clothing.

The children walked barefoot on old silage, all but Adam. Beth placed the inside out muskrat skins on Adam's feet to keep them warm while his shoes dried. We were learning to survive with whatever we could find.

Chapter 23
A New Source of Food

Though no fuel could be found at the Amish home, we stocked one wagon half full of vegetables harvested from their garden. Onions and tubers would add to any meat we could find along the road. Our route took us in a rural direction. Few Amish lived on the fast lane. Their gardens proved more important than travelling. Waiting for help to come to us while food was at our disposal was the obvious choice and unanimously agree upon.

The Mennonites were easily found once we knew what to look for. Their tractors with metal wheels made angled marks in the pavement along the side of the road. We eventually tracked one to an underground tank besides the burnt foundation of a barn. It held more diesel than we could put in the large tank we carried.

Days blended into weeks, though none of us could be sure exactly what day or time it was. Days were measured between sleeping and eating. Our eating habits adapted to eating two meals a day.

We were only putting about twenty hours into what we called a day. With no sunshine, it was impossible to tell the difference. We merely survived one day to the next. Collecting wood became a large part of our daily chores. The temperature dipped lower every day.

One time when Marcos and I were collecting water and wood, we heard a splash in the swamp. It sounded like a flat stone had been thrown into the water.

"What was that?" Marcos asked. "There's somebody over there." He pointed in the dark.

Marcos' voice initiated something to make a second splash out in the void.

I knew that sound could only have been made by a beaver, slapping its tail on the water to give a warning. I had heard it hundreds of times before. It surprised me because I thought that all animals bigger than a cat were dead. "Marcos, give me that torch." We were saving the flashlights. "We're going for a little walk. I'm going to show you something neat. We'll set the wood down here and pick it up when we come back."

"Who threw that rock in the water?" the boy asked.

I'm sure Marcos had never seen animals wilder than those held captive in the zoo. "It was a beaver. He slapped his tail on the water to warn the other beavers about us." I felt like I was the narrator of some nature show.

"There's more than one of them?" His voice cracked. I could tell he wasn't even sure what a beaver was.

"I hope so." I had eaten beaver before, and we could all use some more fresh meat. I knew I could trap one if I could find where it had been living.

"Do they bite?" His ignorance of the animal made me laugh.

"Only if you're made of poplar. You are a real boy aren't you, Pinocchio?" I'm sure he had no idea what I was talking about. I laughed again. "No they won't bite unless you're made of wood. That's what they eat. Poplar is a wood with a soft bark. Some people call it aspen." Now I was a botanist. I was starting to laugh at myself too.

"What are they eating now that all the wood is burned?" Marcos asked a good question this time.

"That's what we're going to find out. Follow me and be careful not to fall into the water." It looked deep along the edge.

I held the torch up, and to my surprise, noticed that the poplar trees out in the water weren't burned. Their top parts were, but the lower half near the water was undamaged. Their waxy bark remained unscorched near water level.

"Ya know, Marcos, this is going to make our life a little easier. Did you know that beavers store their food underwater, so that they can eat it in the winter?" Another source of food just became evident. Beavers had lived and might continue to survive for a while.

We walked along the edge of the slow meandering riverbank until we came to an area that felt as if it was hollow beneath our feet, a pile of wood covered by earth and mud. We were standing over a beaver den in the bank of the river.

My concentration was interrupted by Marcos bouncing up and down on the unstable ground.

"Be careful, we could fall through and land in a nest of beavers," I warned.

Marcos immediately stopped jumping on nature's trampoline, and stood frozen in terror, as if his next move would be his last.

I laughed yet again. "'Don't worry, it'll hold you. Beavers are nature's engineers. They built this lodge to hold snow that weighs more than us, but don't jump on it anyway. I don't want to scare them away now that we know where they live. I took off my backpack and took out copper wire I'd kept from a cellar we ransacked. The longest piece I had was only about seven feet long. I would have liked it better if it had been a bit longer.

I made a loop on one end and tied the other end to roots down at the water's edge. Marcos held the torch as I lowered myself to water level. It was too dark to see, so I had to feel for the entrance to the lodge. I was justifiably nervous about putting my arm down into this water. I told Marcos that beavers didn't bite, but I'm sure one would, defending its lodge.

I found the tunnel going in, and centered the snare with a couple of sticks that were lying in the water. Now any beaver going in or out would pull the wire tight around its neck, and we'd have fresh meat tomorrow. Getting back up from setting the snare was more difficult than I expected. My age was catching up with me.

"Let's get our wood and then tell the others what we're going to have for breakfast tomorrow." Anticipation sent chills up my spine. I hadn't had these feelings since I was kid on opening night of trapping season.

We loaded all the wood we could find onto the trailer and headed back to the rest with the good news.

That night I couldn't sleep thinking how happy everyone would be with meat that wasn't turtle or muskrat, so I stayed up and kept the fire going. It needed to be bigger all the time as it was getting colder. We had plenty of wood. The trailer made it easier to gather large amounts of wood without constantly returning to drop off the small bundles. We only had to make one trip.

While the others slept I sat and thought about our new discovery. I'm surprised I didn't wake the others with my growling stomach. I couldn't wait any longer. I went to wake Marcos. He was already awake.

"Are we going now Nick?" he slept about as much as I did.

"Yea, you go get some more wire and I will get the truck ready to go."

"Do you think that we got him?"

"I bet we did, but bring the wire and we'll set some more snares."

We went our separate ways. I unhooked the trailer so we could move faster, and filled up the Hyster with diesel. The fuel gauge didn't work, so I was leaving nothing to chance.

Marcos came running up to the road trailing a tangled mess of copper wire behind him.

"Do you want to drive?" I asked, knowing what the answer would be.

"Yeah. I'll drive if you want me to." He was really awake now.

I helped him into the seat. "Put on your seat belt, and tighten it up. If I would have had mine on the day we went into the crater, I wouldn't have gotten a concussion."

I stood on the edge of the truck with one foot in the step, so I could jump off if I had to. Marcos was a good fork truck driver—foot right to the floor all the time. I would tell him to slow down and he would, but after about thirty seconds we would be at full throttle again. Luckily the company had placed governors on the throttle, so top speed was about eight miles an hour. I would disconnect it when I was driving but left it on when Marcos drove.

Soon we were pulling up to the edge of the swamp.

"Don't get off the blacktop, we'll get stuck again."

Making sure the brake was on, we abandoned the truck and hurried down to where the swamp turned into a winding river. The light of the torch made it easy to see, but finding the place where we set the trap wasn't. We walked back and forth the same stretch of river over and over again, but couldn't find the entrance.

"Maybe we walked by it; let's go back and start again." I turned to head back to the swamp, when I saw Marcos bouncing on the bank. "Hey, you're going to fall in," I yelled.

"Is this it Nick?" he asked.

"Could be, let's check and see. Here hold this." I handed him the torch. "Hold it lower to the ground." I knelt down to look for the snare I had set. The poor lighting made it difficult to find the wire in the tangle of roots and branches beneath the water line. Feeling more than seeing, I found the entrance to the lodge: an opening in the bank about six inches below the waterline.

I felt for the wire on the roots above the water, because that's where I had anchored it. Finding nothing, I began looking underwater. It was possible that with all the precipitation the water had risen. My hand touched something sharp, like a piece of wire, almost cutting my palm. Carefully I reached back to the same area. I was poked again. I felt from the tip of the wire, up into the lodge. I was sure our meal was dead, lying on the floor of the den. The wire was lodged on some roots. I reached up into the entrance hole to untangle the wire, when I felt the wire go slack. A sudden jolt went from my left arm to my neck, like an electric shock. I was pulled towards the water. Before I knew it, I was submerged. The snare kinked and wrapped around my little finger. The animal's tail paddled my body as it tried to escape. Apparently the snare had wrapped around the front leg and neck of the rodent, preventing a quick death.

Marcos attempted to rescue me and fell into the water with me. The beaver continued heading for deeper water, dragging me further away from the surface. Marcos thrashed, but could not swim. I had to act fast to save us both. I pulled hard on the copper wire, which only brought the toothy critter closer to my face. I pulled as hard as I could. My lungs burned for air. Another strong tug and I broke free. As my head broke the surface I swallowed air and water at the same time. I immediately looked for Marcos. He struggled to hold roots along the river's bank. The smell of castor drifted heavy on the water as I swam to the edge. I struggled to climb the muddy embankment. With Marcos' assistance, and the never-ending will to live, I did.

In the turmoil of falling into the water, the pain that I should have sensed was absent. My little finger had been amputated from the small knuckle down; blood ran down my wrist. The copper wire wasn't strong enough to hold an adult beaver, but it was strong enough to tear off my finger.

Breakfast had gotten away and it took my little pinky with it; but now we knew where it lived.

Chapter 24
Thanks, but No Thanks

We traveled an estimated two hundred miles south: shelter to shelter, swamp to swamp, garden to garden, and tank to tank, occasionally picking through rubble for supplies needed. Cold weather followed. There was still no sun to warm the air in the day; clouds blocked its life-giving rays. We'd stay in an area as long as the meat held out. We were eating a lot better since we'd learned to trap for food. Soon fresh meat was part of our daily menu. Every stream, meandering river, or swamp would be explored. Less traveling used less fuel.

On one trip between shelters, we stopped near a bridge to eat. The turtles we collected were to be the main course. Because of the cold weather, they seldom moved, and we wanted to eat them while they were still fresh. One could die, and we wouldn't even be able to tell. I was in the mood for something different anyway.

I butchered the reptiles and threw them in a pot with potatoes and carrots and onions. As they simmered, the aroma coming out of the kettle wasn't what I was expecting. The lobster-like sweetness we had anticipated was substituted by a very fishy odor. A scum developed at the top of the stew. I skimmed most of it off, but could do nothing about the smell. Steam enveloped all who stood by the fire to warm themselves.

"That smells horrible. How in the hell are we going to eat that?" Sarah waved her hand in front of her nose. "All we did with those stinking turtles was to waste the potatoes and carrots. Nobody is going to eat any of that."

I had to agree with her. I have eaten many different things, but was willing to go hungry tonight.

No matter how long it cooked, the odor lingered. The vegetables were getting mushy so we figured: this was the best it was going to get. We ladled half a bowl each just to try it. We all blew on the steaming meal.

I took a taste of the meat, very chewy with a distinct fishy taste. I blew in and out to cool it faster. It was burning my mouth.

"Take your time. Nobody is going to take it from you," Beth said.

Sarah continued to cool her share.

Maria was busy saying grace. "Thank you Lord for this food I am about to receive." She did stir the concoction and immediately returned her hands to a praying position. "Please protect us from sickness while we consume your blessing. Amen."

"You've got to be kidding me," Beth said. "You would give thanks to a God who you think caused this whole thing, especially when this is looking you in the eye?" The angry atheist spooned the stew high enough above her bowl to give Maria a good look at the slop we were about to eat.

"We wouldn't have this if God hadn't led us to it. Everything that has happened is his will. He didn't cause it, but did allow it to happen for a reason that we aren't meant to understand." Maria took out one of her last remaining cigarettes and lit it up. The conversation went silent as she savored the initial puff. The cherry of her smoke wiggled as she shook. "And if I want to thank him, I'm going to!" Smoke billowed out of her mouth as she spoke.

"And you say it was your God's will that all those we knew and loved burned to death? Are you still going to hold on to those old stories? What happened here is a natural occurrence. This happened sixty-five million years ago. Now it has happened again. God had nothing to do with it. Did your God do this same thing to get rid of the dinosaurs? Sorry Maria but I just can't buy it." Her hands shook as she blew on her lunch. "We just fucked up and stopped looking for shit. The politicians are the ones to blame. They're the ones who cut NASA's budget. Was this God's long-term plan to punish mankind? Bullshit!" Her stew went into the fire.

Steam rose from the embers, it hissed and snapped while the rest of us went silent. "Come on Marcos; let's go get some more wood while we're near water." I had heard Beth's rants before, and looked for any excuse to escape another one.

"I'm not done eating yet." He helped himself to a second bowl. "I caught the biggest one didn't I? That's why it tastes so good. Thanks for teaching me how to catch 'em, Beth."

"Bring it with you." I threw my stew in the fire and walked down to the water's edge.

Chapter 25
On Foot

The wind blew the cold rain in under the roof of the fork truck. The stinging precipitation turned to sleet.

The flat wheels of the high lift weren't meant for anything other than concrete floors; any ice or snow would leave us stranded. We decided to make a run for it and head as far south as our fuel would take us. Two of the cars were scuttled to eliminate the whipping effect at full throttle. Getting away from the snow was imperative.

Driving wide open and non-stop was more than the machine could muster. We took another step back in time the day we left the fork and trailer combo dead in a pool of its own life fluids.

All the tools were left behind, except a couple adjustable wrenches and screwdrivers. The cans of diesel had to stay, so we made as many torches as we could carry. Every pocket was filled with tubers. Even the children toted a couple of carrots or a tater or two. Each adult wore as many uniforms as possible while still being able to walk. The beaver furs we had collected were heavy and cumbersome to carry, but they were the only bedding we had. We were now on foot.

Torches soaked in diesel lit the way. Cattail reeds were dried, soaked with fuel oil, then wrapped tightly around a metal handle, then again wrapped tightly with copper wire, more reeds, then more wire. When it was finished it resembled a beehive with a hole at the top. They gave off a greenish-blue light, but lasted longer than any we had designed to this point.

The sleet turned to snow. The flakes grew bigger as the wind increased. We wandered along with no real plan or sense of direction due to the blizzard conditions. We all followed the person carrying the torch, and sometimes even the lead person wouldn't know where the road was. More than once the shell of a car or truck would appear out of the whiteout, and we came to a screeching halt.

We discussed taking shelter in cars along the highway, but nobody cared for the idea of sharing a vehicle with a crispy corpse.

The precipitation had caused the rivers to swell. The sound of running water could be heard.

Sarah, who was leading at the time, held up the torch. She looked over the guardrails and yelled, "Hey, there's a dry place. And look! There's already some wood stuck in the end."

We were all wet from the sticky, dime-sized snow. I was willing to take anything now. The idea of wood I didn't have to gather appealed to me as well.

I was blinded by the light of Sarah's torch, so walked to the right of her to get my own perspective. I looked over the edge and found the source of the water. A big drainage tile was emptying water into a river. A couple of feet higher and to the right was a second concrete tile, about six feet in diameter. It had been displaced during the earthquake, enough so that all the water flowed into the other tile. The sudden cessation of flowing water apparently had left debris at the exit point. It looked safe enough. There was no reason for me to believe that our combined weight would cause it to collapse. The water was clearly diverted to the tunnel on the left. "I think this is home for the night...as far as I'm concerned, looks safe enough," I said.

"Looks good to me too," Beth said, carrying Tara in her left arm and brushing snow off the baby's hair with her right.

"Me too," voiced Maria.

"Let's get out of this snow before the kids catch pneumonia." Sarah climbed over the railing and started down the embankment before we could have any more discussion.

"Be careful, those rocks will be slippery." I followed her to watch out for her safety. "Slow down and wait for the rest of us to help you with the kids."

Just as I expected, Sarah slipped on a wet rock, and fell on another pile five to seven feet below. She was carrying both Adam and Megan.

We saw the torch land on the rocks with a blaze of sparks that temporally blinded the rest of us.

Once our vision returned, we followed the crying down to where all three of them lay. I struggled with my backpack to get the flashlights out.

Megan was the first we found. She was the one crying. I held the light while Beth did a quick triage on the toddler. Her leg was twisted in an awkward position.

"Looks like a possible broken tibia and fibula," she said as she handed Megan up to Maria, who had climbed down below me.

I shined the light up at the guardrails along the road and saw Marcos holding Tara and Eve. Their combined weight was more than his, but he was balancing both of them on his hips so they could see over the railing.

"I need that light, Nick," Beth yelled.

I swung back to point the beam at her voice. She held her second patient up so she could see into his ears.

Even I could see that Adam was in dire straits. My training in the fire department had taught me that fluid coming out of the ears is not a good sign.

Beth carried Adam up to the road herself. She set him down and turned her attention to Megan.

Sarah was getting up on her own, though she obviously was in some distress. She started to vomit. The pain she was experiencing, because of the injury to her shins, was overwhelming. When she fell on the rocks, she did everything she could to protect the kids, so her shins, and her back, took the majority of the impact.

I helped Sarah over the guardrail. "You should have waited," I said, showing no bedside manner. I was not the type of person to be in the care giving field. I'd struggled with showing compassion while I was in the fire service.

Beth looked up. "Nick, we have to get a fire started and get out of this snow, now!" She was doing a secondary assessment on Adam, who wasn't making a sound, he just lay there unconscious.

"Let's all head down into the dry culvert. I can't get a fire going until we all get inside." I wanted the fire to be on the edge of the opening to let the smoke escape to the outside.

Marcos was doing a great job keeping the other kids quiet and out of the way, but I had a more important job for him to do. "Marcos, let Sarah watch Tara and Eve. I need you to take the hatchet and this flashlight, gather as much wood as you can, and bring it over to that culvert opening. We're going to need a ton of it. Follow your tracks back." He ran off immediately, gathering wood as he was told.

"C'mon, help me get him down there." Beth then raised her voice so the rest could hear. "Let's all head down and get out of this snow. Marcos, drop what you're doing and help us get the babies down these rocks."

I saw the flashlight move in the telltale fashion that told me he was running.

I picked up Sarah's torch and relit it. Just a spark from the now empty lighter would ignite the smoldering fuel-soaked reeds. Now I had something to light the fire. It would take a lot of heat to get it going, because the wood was wet to begin with.

Forming a chain, with Marcos and myself to assist the others where the most difficult walking was, we carefully climbed up into the concrete tube.

Chapter 26
Tragedy Leads to New Hope

The group went further into the culvert than I did to escape the snow. The fire was my main concern. "Marcos, thank you for the help with the kids," I had to shout to overpower the thundering sound of the water gushing out of the other culvert. "Now can you get me some more wood, everything you can find?"

The beam of his flashlight was growing dimmer. The batteries were just about spent. I couldn't give him the torch because I needed it to start the fire.

I turned my attention to the pile of wood. Something caught my eye. It almost looked like it had been piled. Under the wet wood on top, I discovered remnants of wood that had been burned. I didn't have time to think about it, I had to get the fire started as soon as possible. We were all wet and freezing.

One of the cans I kept in my backpack contained dry tinder I'd collected along the way. With that and the torch, the fire slowly started to catch and illuminate the inside of the culvert. The smoke was pulled outside as I had anticipated.

Marcos ran up to the entrance. "Is this enough?" He dropped a small armful near the fire. There was more snow than wood.

"We're going to need a whole bunch more than that. Here take the torch now, I'm through with it."

Marcos gladly took the torch and said, "The batteries are almost dead in the flashlight anyways." We only had one flashlight left, and we were saving that. He took the torch and headed out on his mission.

I took the batteries out of the flashlight and placed the plastic strategically in the fire. The plastic would melt and continue to burn for a long period of time, giving the fire all the help it could get. I placed other pieces of wood near the fire to dry. Once it was going on its own, I could go check on Adam and Megan.

I walked around the others towards the back of the culvert. I needed to know if it was safe to spend the night. We couldn't afford to have the water rise and flush us out. The pitch was noticeably going down the further I went into the pipe. The tunnel was long enough that I couldn't see. The light of the fire didn't reach the back.

"Your fire's going out," Beth yelled to me as I walked by.

She was busy making a splint for Megan's leg out of whatever she could find.

I looked back to see that she was right. Investigating my fire, I found that the snow from the outside was melting and running down into the coals at the bottom, putting it out. "Damn it," I said, scrambling to save my fire. I carefully placed every piece of burning wood next to another one, up and away from the trickle of water now starting to find its way down to the others. The culvert was working just as it was designed. It was moving water from a high point to a low point, however not in the direction the engineers planned.

We could position ourselves to remain dry, but this would put each of us in an uncomfortable position, lying, or sitting at an angle, always leaning.

I kept the fire going thanks to the melted plastic of the flashlight. It took a while before I could leave the fire untended, since the mist from the other culvert kept everything damp.

Marcos continued to gather wood. He didn't whimper or whine once, even after four or five trips.

Once the fire climbed beyond the point it was before the water trickled in, it began to throw off some heat. Some of the wood had started to dry out. Everyone came over to the warmth—everyone except Beth, Maria, and Adam.

"You better bring him over to the fire and keep him warm. I'm going back in here to look things over," I said as I straddled Maria's feet to get around, heading to the back again to inspect.

"We're going with you." Beth held the torch up. Her eyes looked at me, then at Adam, then back up to me.

I knew Adam was dead. Without saying a word, Maria, Beth and I took Adam, if that was even his name, to the back of the tunnel. We laid him down and put some cloth over his little face to keep the dirt off. Maria took a small toy car out of his pocket and put it in his hand. We all took the fresh dirt that had fallen from the opening at the top of the culvert and covered him so rats wouldn't devour his body, at least not while we were there.

While I was inspecting the opening above Adam's shameful resting place, Maria built drying racks out of the wood Marcos had been delivering. The racks would dry our clothing while we had wood enough for a big fire.

Sarah didn't know about Adam, she had been busy taking the wet clothing off the other children to dry them. They were cold and crying. She barked at Beth, "Better give me another one of those, for Megan."

Beth had already given Megan a five-hundred milligram painkiller.

"Give her one so she can sleep." Sarah held out her hand.

Beth lashed out, "Forever... just what did you do in pediatrics for Dr. Stone? Are you sure you worked with children? There's already one dead, let's not shoot for two." Her bottom lip quivered.

Sarah took Beth's tirade with all the blame intended to go with it, now that she realized that Adam was dead. She began to weep.

"Let's try and get everyone dried out while we have enough wood for the fire." I didn't want to get involved. I was as mad as Beth was at Sarah for rushing down that embankment.

Marcos had hauled enough wood to keep the fire going for an hour or two. I knew we would need more than he could carry alone. I was going to have to help.

"Marcos, come on up here and get dried off. Stand next to the fire a while. I'll go get some too. While I'm gone, you're the man. Keep the fire going, put some wood beside it to dry, and don't play with it. I'll be right back."

I made my way down the slippery rocks then back up to the road. I walked a distance before gathering any wood. Marcos had cleaned up most of it near the culvert.

I walked further than I intended. I started flipping over steel roofing, hoping to find wood Marcos had missed. The weather didn't help matters. Anything I found was soaked with wet snow.

I was surprised that Marcos had found any wood at all. The cellars that usually had some wood left over along their edges were just pits of ash and rusting metal. Normally one would have to be careful not to step on nails. It almost looked like it had been picked over, though we hadn't come across any other people.

I made several trips, returning with less wood each time. I had contributed far less than Marcos had. I didn't have the stamina anymore, but then he was forty-two years younger than me.

I wasn't comfortable quitting. I wanted to be with Beth. I knew the accident with Adam wasn't setting well with her.

I ventured out into the snow one more time to gather as much wood as my old bones could carry. The tracks Marcos had made earlier were almost filled in from all the snow that was now coming down. I took a course that led me away from where Marcos or I had been. I didn't dare stray too far. My torch was getting low, and my tracks were filling in fast too.

I came to a truck that had been on an exit ramp. Like any other vehicle we'd found, most of it had burned, except for the box and its cargo. It had been one of those refrigerated home delivery trucks, the ones with the good ice cream. Apparently the temperature of the refrigerated food, and type of insulation the box was built from, helped prevent its total destruction. The back half of the truck was still intact, minus the tires. What struck me was the fact that all the doors to the frozen food compartments were open.

Nobody would have opened those doors during the chaos of that day. People were doing everything not to catch on fire. Nobody wanted to loot tutti-frutti ice cream.

I hurried back with the few charred boards I'd found. No longer looking for wood, but anxious to find other survivors and tell Beth the news, I tossed the three planks, and began to run back to the culvert.

I approached the opening to the emergency shelter with the same caution I had used when I left, even though my adrenaline was much higher coming in than it had been going out. Carefully taking one step at a time, I heard yelling over the din of the rushing water from the other culvert. I continued my cautious rate of navigation, picking each rock I would step on and how I would plan my step to the next. My heart said run, my instinct said slow down, survive.

Looking up over the fire I saw that Beth and Maria were arguing with Sarah. All three were crying and yelling at the same time.

I stepped around the fire, and over the kids warming themselves, down to the women. "Stop it," I barked. "This isn't going to change anything. Adam is gone. We're still alive, and I'm going to keep it that way." I didn't raise my voice often, but when I did, it caught people's attention.

All three went silent.

"Listen, I think there are some more survivors. I found signs of activity after the fire. There was a truck that somebody had opened the doors on. We all need to go out and look for wood and signs of people. Sarah, are you able to walk and help us?"

She struggled to get up. "Yes I can still walk... I think."

"Even if we don't find anybody we can stay undercover here until the snow lets up, but we'll need more wood. No more arguing. We need to work as a team. What's done is done. Let's go." I wasn't waiting for a response. "Marcos you stay here and watch the little ones. Get dried out and try to get them to sleep. We'll be back before the wood runs out." It would be futile to tell him an hour or two.

"Where's Adam?" Marcos asked. He was old enough to know the truth, but I didn't want to take the time to deal with that now.

"Listen to me." I looked him right in the eye and said, "Adam was hurt very bad. He died and is in the back of the tunnel. I don't want any of you going back there. Do you understand? I'll talk to you about it when we get back. Now I expect you to be in charge here. I know I can count on you, right?"

"Yes." He had a solemn look on his face while he held Tara and Eve, both staring into the fire. Megan was asleep. The pill had taken effect.

The four of us left the entrance in single file. The tension was thicker than the snow, but I knew it would quit snowing.

Chapter 27
New Hope Leads to Tragedy.

We split up and fanned out to cover more area. Beth and Sarah needed to talk to each other. Constant communication was the only way to insure we wouldn't get separated.

The open doors of the truck were the only sign there were any survivors. No tracks in the snow or signs of fires could be found.

Snow covered the ground, obscuring any wood. Small pieces were scattered. There was little under the steel roofing, like there was in other towns. The trees that were left were just stumps lacking any limbs within reach.

The snow was still falling heavily. Our tracks had all but filled in and were difficult to recognize. Dragging a piece of metal roofing, piled with wet wood, we made it back to the culvert.

It took us longer than I'd expected. Looking down at the culvert, no glow from the fire could be seen. It had either gone out because Marcos ran out of wood, or because it was too wet.

Forming a type of bucket brigade, we carefully moved the fuel from our sleigh to the culvert.

A few coals glowed in the smoldering fire. Water bubbled out of each piece. Steam rose above the charred wood to the round ceiling and then out into the night.

Night, I'm so tired of that word. I laughed to myself while watching the steam mix with the snowflakes falling almost out of nowhere.

With the dim light of the fire at my back, I looked out to where a city once stood. I stepped to the edge of the culvert away from the steam, smoke, and snow into an ultimate blackness. I imagined this was what it was like to be blind. I could hear the rushing water. A vision of city lights popped into my mind's eye. I could almost imagine car lights traveling along the interstate, forming a never ending snake of white and red lights. Then I realized this view would never be seen again, except in visions.

I turned my attention back to the fire. It took a long time to get to the point that a person could warm himself. I spent most of my time drying out the wood, clothes, shoes, and manning the fire.

The others were huddled together under some beaver pelts. We only had four, so not everyone had something to cover up with. To make matters worse, they were stiff, not pliable, and didn't have much of an R-value.

We gathered enough wood this time to warm the whole tunnel.

Beth and Sarah hadn't talked since we returned, until now.

"Let Megan under the fur!" Beth yelled in a tone that I hadn't heard since I learned not to do the things that made her yell that way. "I don't care if you freeze to death. We'll drag you back there with Adam. And where's the rest of the pills? You better not have given her more!"

"Fuck you, you fat bitch. I didn't have any..."

"Hey, enough!" I attacked Sarah, even though Beth was just as out of line.

Both screamed obscenities at each other while I thought about what Sarah had said. "Fat bitch." Beth was not fat anymore; none of us were.

Beth started getting up, and then so did Sarah. The beaver pelts flew like Frisbees as the women jumped to their feet. Both were holding children. Both were fuming. As rage burned in each of their hearts, the discipline of their art again showed itself. Each of them laid down the child they were holding with the utmost care.

This break in the tension gave me enough time to intervene. I stepped between the two hotheads in time to stop Sarah from getting her ass kicked. Beth is a better friend than an enemy.

Sarah could hardly walk let alone take on Beth. "Nick, get to fuck out of my way! You're always taking her side on everything. This is between her and me."

"Everybody sit down and calm down," I said. "We need to work as a team now more than ever. This fighting isn't going to bring Adam back."

There wasn't enough room for either to pass. After a few more verbal insults, they both sat down in their original positions.

The adults hadn't slept for an extended period. Caring for the children, gathering wood, and the stress of the day took its toll. Beth, Tara, Maria, Eve, and Marcos were all huddled together under two pelts. Sarah and Megan were on the other side, curled up under the two smallest of the furs.

I was the keeper of the fire until Beth or Marcos woke up, then I might be relieved for a couple of hours. Until then I would have to take cat naps between stoking the fire.

Even with the constant roar of the lower culvert's cascade, I found my brief naps evolving into lengthy periods of deep sleep. I would wake to see the fire nearly out. After putting more wood on the fire and moving wood around the fire to dry, I would doze off again.

My dreams were different than the dreams I had before the days of darkness began. Now I dreamt of torchlight days and endless nights. Sometimes I would dream of those two girls and their dad. Not often enough about the grandbabies, but when I did it was too often, because it reminded me that we'd never see them again. Those dreams were my new nightmares.

Over the roar of the water, the screams of both Sarah and Beth woke me from a dream so deep that I felt I was there, but for the life of me I can't remember what I was dreaming about. It took me a second or two to gain my full senses.

"Where's Megan? Where's Megan?" Sarah was running around the fire, which was nearly out again, stopping short of the end of the culvert, nearly falling.

"You were supposed to be watching her. You should never have been allowed to be with children. If she's hurt in any way I'll kill you myself!" Beth was furious.

"Beth shut up! How to hell did you lose a baby with a broken leg in a tunnel?" I too was questioning Sarah's lack of responsibility.

The women looked around frantically at the entrance and around the rocks, while I went back to where Adam was buried. The piece of burning wood I brought with me was useless as a source of light. I had to dig out the last flashlight.

I walked the length of the narrow passageway to the final resting place of Adam. The instant I approached the pile of loosely mounded dirt, I noticed that it had been disturbed. Snow had found its way into the back of the culvert, but it hadn't just fallen there, it had been brought in and ground into the dirt. I suspected that Megan might have crawled out the widened opening. Upon further investigation I found Adam's body was missing. I began to panic. Could some animal have come in and dragged his little body off? Was that the same fate that fell on Megan?

The opening was too small for me to squeeze through, though a smaller person might be able to. I would have to go around from the other side where the girls were looking.

Beth yelled over the noise of the water, "Did you find her? There's no sign of her down here, there are no tracks at all."

"Where's Sarah?"

"She's looking downstream," she said as she kept looking amongst the rocks.

"You gather up everyone and get the little ones ready to travel. I'll be back soon," I said as I climbed up to where she could hear me. I looked back to make sure she understood what I had said. "Get everyone ready to travel!"

The snow was slippery and I had trouble getting footing. Eventually I reached level ground.

Reaching the other side, it was easy to see tracks coming from the opening near where the water had been diverted. They weren't the tracks I was expecting to see. These tracks were made by humans.

I followed the tracks for a short distance until I came to a large area covered with blood, more blood than I have ever witnessed from any deer that I had harvested. It could have only come from Megan.

I grew nauseous at the thought that other humans could have done this to a child. From the amount of blood that was on the ground, I was sure that there was no use looking for the two children. I hurried back to the entrance and prepared to tell the others of the children's fate.

Before I could speak, Sarah yelled out, "Did you find her? I looked all along the river."

"Marcos," I said, "you stay here and watch Tara and Eve. Maria, Sarah, and Beth, come with me."

The four of us went to the far end of the tunnel. I pointed out the hole that the two kids were taken out from, and explained what I had seen.

"We've got to try and rescue her." Sarah tried to push her way by me.

I described the amount of blood that I had found, and told her I thought looking for her would be futile if not dangerous for the rest of us.

"We can't just leave her," she pleaded

"These are desperate people, willing to do anything to survive. We need to leave this place if the rest of us are going to survive. We're going to stick to the country where there are less people and less competition for food. This place has been picked over, and the survivors are resorting to cannibalism. We need to leave while they're still feeding, and then our tracks will have time to fill in." I looked at Beth and said, "Get the others ready to go now!"

We were out of food, and I didn't have any idea where we were going to get our next meal. We would have to travel in the dark. I knew that whoever snuck in while we were sleeping would be back looking for another easy snack.

Our party left the temporary shelter without another one in mind. We ventured off into the blizzard, blind to our future.

Chapter 28
Confrontation

Days turned into weeks, and weeks melded into months. The weather continued to be colder and fires were needed all the time. Snow was unheard of this far south, but we struggled through it. The kids loved it because they got to ride on a steel roofing toboggan, and throw snowballs at the rest of us. I was usually Marcos' prime target. The snow had advantages that accompanied the cold. It was a fresh source of water. When banked along the sides of shelters, it held out the wind. Its presence made tracking and scouting easier.

Gathering wood for the fire became the most important job next to trapping meat. This task belonged to Marcos and me. The best picking was at the water's edge. The wood was surrounded by water during the initial firestorm, and was spared the heat of any tinder lying under it. The only problem was that we had to go out into the water to get it. This was the same place the beavers were cutting down the remaining trees for their food.

One day while gathering wood I waded out knee deep to retrieve a large limb. I was being careful not to step into a hole and become submersed. We were too far away from the fire, and it was too cold to be soaking wet. I was paying more attention to where I was stepping, than I was about my surroundings.

"Hey, Nick, look. Here comes somebody," Marcos whispered.

I quickly looked up and saw a light flash on and off, and it was coming our way. Immediately I thrust the torch down into the water to extinguish the flame and told Marcos to hide behind a tree stump.

The light came back on and headed our way. My torch must have alerted them to us.

The hatchet that I kept for cutting wood was our only weapon.

"Marcos, go hide that way and don't go back to the others until you know it's safe. Make sure they don't follow you. Stay close enough to see if it's okay." I kept as quiet as I could, but I needed to make sure that he didn't inadvertently lead these strangers to the others should they be the type that took Adam and Megan. "Just like you did with Mick and the others."

He scurried off into the darkness, while I waited to see if these strangers were a threat. I could tell that there were only two, both men.

I was torn between hiding, and confronting them. They had about a couple of hundred yards to go before they reached me.

"Hello, hello! Is anybody there?" shouted one of the men as they approached.

I kept quiet and held my position.

"Show yourself. We saw your light," said the other one.

I hadn't been successful taking on two adversaries before. Now I was even weaker, but I didn't have diarrhea anymore. I didn't feel threatened from these two.

As they drew closer, I could tell that the light was coming from the top of a helmet, worn by one of the two.

"Hello," I said as I stepped out into the beam of his headlamp.

"Freeze!" the other one said, as he pointed a shotgun at me.

I hadn't noticed the gun upon their approach. The beam of his light temporarily blinded me.

"Hey, hey! You don't need to do that, I'm not going to hurt you," I said, hiding the hatchet behind my back.

Calculating my odds, I confessed, "I've got a small ax, but I'm not going to use it as a weapon, I just use it to cut wood." I was nearly up to them, but I wasn't ready to drop it.

"Is there anybody else with you?" One of them asked.

"No. I'm all there is left. Everyone else is dead." I wanted to protect the others just in case these guys were a threat. "I would appreciate it if you would put the gun down. I'm not going to attack you." I figured that I could talk to them now. For one thing, talking is all I have facing a shotgun, and second, if they hadn't shot me by then they weren't going to.

"Where are you from?" asked the one holding me at gunpoint.

"New York State," I responded.

"Where in New York?" he asked as he slowly lowered the weapon.

Until he put down the gun, I wasn't fully cooperating. "It doesn't even exist anymore, it doesn't matter, and I'm trying to forget it. You?"

"We're from Kentucky. You sure have walked a long distance all alone," said the one with the headlamp.

"Got to keep moving to find enough food. Decided to head south to get away from the cold," I said. I was having a difficult time concentrating on their questions due to the fact that I could hear Marcos behind me. I was sure that they had heard him too. There were no leaves to rustle around in, but he had stepped on a stone wall and two rocks had clacked together.

"Is somebody there?" Up came the gun again. "You told me you were alone."

"Put down the gun, he's just a kid." I yelled, "Marcos, come over here and stand by me."

Marcos appeared from the once lush forest, now just a sporadic few stumps of only the biggest trees, charred and void of branches, not much to hide behind. He walked up to me and grabbed my hand in reassurance, much like my grandchildren once did.

I was no longer the threat that they thought I was at the beginning. I had been traveling with a child, and hadn't eaten him. I couldn't be too menacing. The gun was once again lowered.

"This is Marcos. We're gathering wood to keep the rest of our party warm." I wasn't sure that I could trust them, but then on the other hand, it would be nice to have more help gathering wood and food.

"How many more are in your group?" asked the one with the light, as he shined it directly in my face.

I wasn't entirely ready to tell them that we had women in the group; I needed to feel them out a little more.

"Help Marcos and me get a bunch of wood and I'll introduce you to all of them. My name's Nick, again this is Marcos." I reached out my hand to shake theirs.

The one with the light held out his hand. "My name's Pete, and this is George." The big guy turned to his buddy, "I mean Jorge."

I shook Pete's hand and noticed he had a powerful grip. He was a big man.

I reached to shake the hand of the other man. Even though the light was away from his face I could see a smile develop into a full-blown toothy grin.

I no longer distrusted these two. The handshake made me feel this man was trustworthy. The smile was sincere; I could trust the other one too.

Chapter 29

Getting to Know One Another

The makeshift sleigh we had used to haul the children now carried wood. More effort was needed to drag it, since the wood weighed more than a couple of toddlers. Both men cooperated and gathered wood without speaking. It seemed good to fill up the sled in half the time.

I had no choice but to head back to camp. They had done their part, now I would have to make good on my word. My first impressions told me that I could trust them, but I had to be sure. "How do I know that when we get back to the others that you won't kill us all and bring us back to your group?" I hated to be so blunt, but it was only about a quarter mile to the shed, and I didn't have much time to get to know them socially. I knew once we broke over the hill they would see the glow of the fire.

"If we were going to kill you, we would have done it by now. We only use the gun for self defense, so you tell anyone in your party that's interested in starting any shit, that we've killed already and aren't afraid to do it again," Pete said. He had his lamp off, and my torch was all wet and wouldn't light, so I couldn't see his face. Apparently they were used to walking in the dark as well.

Sensing that he didn't quite trust me either, I said, "I can assure you, you have no reason to worry. We have found a way to find food without eating each other, or anybody else. We even have some extra in case you're hungry, but not a lot."

The winds were beginning to pick up again, giving away the location of the others. Jorge yelled out, "You got fresh meat?" as the aroma of supper drifted our way.

We neared the driveway that led to the steel tool shed. "What have you guys been eating?" I asked.

Pete answered for the duo again. "Mostly animal grain from farm silos. Cans of food when we can find them... pretty picked over near the cities. Plus it's too dangerous there. We ate mushrooms until it got cold. There ain't no mushrooms no more."

It struck me funny that I never thought to cut into one of those silos. I'd seen them. I just forgot that they have grain. Apparently the grain in them wasn't as subject to the dampness that molded the corn in other silos. The corn in the steel silos must have been dried before it was stored, while the other corn still had moisture in it.

As we walked down the drive of the farm, no longer recognizable, the talking ceased. We walked past the empty cellar of the once proud home, handed down generation to generation. Past the rusting pickups, tractors, and a combine that was now sitting on equally rusted rims. There was no silo, this was not a farm that raised animals. I wasn't sure what crop they had raised, and there wasn't much machinery that I recognized.

I could hear the now familiar bickering between Beth and Sarah growing louder as we neared the shed—not because we were getting closer, but because their argument was intensifying. Both of them kept their distance when I was around but when I was gone for awhile, then no holds barred.

"Ladies, could you please use your inside voice? We have company," I said as the four of us walked into the light of the fire.

My request was fulfilled with immediate silence.

"Gentlemen, this is our group. These three ladies are all nurses. Beth here is my wife. This is Maria, and this is Sarah."

Both women said, "Hello."

Both men said, "Hi."

"You've met Marcos. Over there under those furs are Tara, and Eve. They're just young children, orphans. And that's it. We had two children taken by cannibals upstate." After that I was temporarily speechless. I regained my composure. "Oh, everyone this is Pete and this is...." I had forgotten his name, I knew it was something Hispanic, but couldn't remember.

"Jorge, Jorge Hernandez," he said, nodding as he looked directly at Maria and smiled.

She returned the smile, but with a far less tooth-to-mouth ratio.

Sarah blurted, "How do you spell that?

"J-O-R-G-E" he said, carefully enunciating each letter.

"Oh, George?" she said.

"See I told ya," said Pete, as he punched the little guy in the arm.

Feeling I was left out of the joke, I said, "There's some beaver jerky if you're hungry." As a host, I had never offered my guests this before and felt kind of funny hearing it out loud. "Eat what you want, there're more swimming around in the swamp."

"Maria made some fresh rat stew... just like Mom used to make," Beth said, barely holding back the laughter.

Then the other two women broke out into uncontrollable laughter.

"Here, have some cattail bread to go with it. Yumm," Maria said sarcastically, rubbing her tummy in a clockwise motion.

Not being a great fan of cattail bread I too started laughing.

Now Tara and Eve were up and wanted to become part of the fun. They each began laughing without even knowing what we were laughing about.

I looked over at Pete and Jorge; the contagious laughter infected everyone.

Jorge's large smile was ever widening as he reached into his backpack. "I have some cow grain," he said.

I don't believe there is a term for the type of humor that was making us laugh, neither irony, nor sarcasm. More some sick type of humor that only can be appreciated if one suffers from post-traumatic stress disorder. In retrospect, it wasn't that funny.

Both men sat down at our fire and ate what we could offer them without complaint or criticism.

Pete took a break from eating and wiped his mouth on what remained of a sleeve. "Thank you for the meal. We haven't had fresh meat besides mice since we killed a coyote about six months or so ago. We've been eating this animal grain. We've still got some more left; it's all yours in appreciation of your hospitality."

"It's our pleasure. You boys said you were from Kentucky?"

"We're both coal miners," Pete said.

Beth spun around, "I thought there weren't any coal mines in operation anymore. I thought coal wasn't used now days.

Pete shook his head. "No, our mine and one other were still in operation, they're harvesting what they can for the World's Contingency Plan. We were at work when it started and we still don't know what to hell is going on. All we know is everyone with a lick of brains is dead. You're the first people we've come across since we decided to go around the cities and stay out in the country. Those left in the cities aren't going to make it. Once they're done feeding on each other, then they'll be dead too, they'll be out of food. Then maybe we can go back in and use what we can."

"You haven't seen military or Red Cross or anything?" Beth asked.

"Nothing. The only other people we've come across attacked us, and I had to kill two of them to keep them from taking George too. They dragged off another guy who survived the mine collapse with us. He was hurt and couldn't fight back. George and I ran for our lives when I almost ran out of shells."

"So you only have one bullet for the gun now?" Sarah said with her usual bitter tone.

"We used that one to kill the coyote. Why else do you think I let George carry it? The gun's just a deterrent." Both he and Jorge laughed. He turned his attention to me. "You seem to be doing quite well. I never thought about catching beavers. I didn't think many other animals made it. I thought the coyote was a freak thing. We didn't dare eat rats, with all the disease and such." He stirred the remainder of the rat stew.

Maria surprised everyone by speaking. "We only eat the rats out in the country, near old farms, never near a city. There must be epidemics in the cities. It didn't seem to be a safe place for the children." She shocked all of us that had been with her through it all. Since I'd known her, I'd never heard her interject. She only spoke when spoken to.

"Were you a nurse too?" asked Jorge.

"Yes, and I still am," she said smiling.

"A very beautiful one too, if you don't mind me saying." Jorge was smiling wide, head down, but looking up in anticipation of her response.

"Not at all. Thank you, Jorge." Maria shyly looked away.

"This stew is the best I ever had too," Jorge said, this time with his head held high.

"Thank you again, Jorge." Maria smiled as wide as he did.

Beth cleared her throat and asked, "Have you heard any planes or helicopters?"

I sensed that she was getting annoyed with their flirting. I guess it had been some time since I'd flirted with Beth, but in these conditions flirting hadn't been on my mind much.

"No, nothing like that," Pete said. "Do you know what happened? It was terrorists, wasn't it?"

"We're not sure of anything, but my best guess is that a meteor or comet hit somewhere, and this is what is left." Beth was the only one in our group who might have a clue.

"They can do that?" Pete asked.

"Scientist's know that was one of the contributing factors that led to the extinction of the dinosaurs. I can see how this would have done it. This would have been enough." She shook her head as she looked off into the darkness.

"Would it be like this all over the world?" Pete asked.

She blew on her hands to warm them. "I don't know. We haven't met anyone with any answers either. It's possible, I guess. I don't know... I hope not."

Chapter 30
Building a Clan

The extra help proved to be invaluable. Wood could be gathered while traps were being set. Now that Pete and Jorge were with us, the chores per person were reduced. We were eating better, and we always had dry wood for the fire.

Before they showed up, sleep was a luxury. When Marcos and I weren't collecting wood, we were setting or checking traps, building shelters, or this or that. There was always a chore to do. When the two of us stumbled on a swamp where the beaver were plentiful, there wasn't time to set and check traps, plus clean the animals and flesh out the firs, so the women took on that grizzly task. Actually, once I showed them how to do it, they became proficient. I found they would save more meat and do a better job fleshing the pelts. This too became part of their daily routine. They also gathered wood around camp, cooked meals and cared for the children.

Once all the work was done, we had time to sit around the fire and talk. It was a big deal that we had new people with new stories and ideas.

They were just as intrigued as we were with new tales. The conversations were split between before and after. This was healing we hadn't had time for before.

Several different topics were discussed around the fire. Often we threw around ideas related to surviving: where to put out traps, new ways to preserve meat, or build torches. This was a good time to plan the workload for the next day.

Sometimes we'd speculate about what civilization would be like in five years. Of course this all depended on how many survived.

When everyone's belly was full, and nobody was thirsty, and everyone was warm, those were the times we began to cherish.

We enjoyed the babies more. Eve was talking, and Tara was a bundle of trouble. Her curiosities were insatiable.

Marcos was more of a man than a child. I don't think we could have made it this far without him. Now he could go back to being a kid.

Once, when we were all sitting around the fire, watching the children, a break came in the sky. We could see sunbeams coming through the clouds at first. Then we caught a glimpse of the sun. Not all of it, just a fraction. That was all it took to make every one of us raise our hands in unison to cover our eyes. The brightness hurt, but we each took a quick peek to reassure ourselves. The moment was the spark that lit the fire of hope.

Fleeting joy was replaced with horror now that we saw the landscape clearly. It looked like ancient black and white photographs of Hiroshima, Nagasaki, or Geneva. Trees with only the largest limbs remained, surrounded by debris. Anything metal was rusted, though no twisted metal could be seen like at the places nuclear bombs were detonated.

Again I saw a water tower in the distance, but this time it wasn't worth the walk. We had learned to sustain our needs without the infrastructure of the past. We'd learned to purify water without relying on artificial aqueducts. We'd learned to find food without going to the nearest 7-11. Our animal instincts, along with the combined knowledge attained through past experiences, brought us to this stage of survival.

We had survived, and would probably continue to survive. We came to the conclusion that we were the beginning of the next age of man. We would have to rebuild the world. Any history recorded from this point backwards would be our responsibility and of our choosing. For the first time in history, the opportunity to change the world for the better, eliminating the mistakes of the past, had been given to one generation. We came to the conclusion that it was better to learn how to live in this world than to keep trying to find the old one.

Chapter 31
The Next Generation.

Time was immeasurable. No sun to differentiate morning from night, no moon to keep track of the months. Although one cycle was ever present.

The birth of Maria's baby came. The child was white, proving that the animal who had raped her at the hospital was Caucasian, at least the one raping her at the moment of conception.

Maria and Jorge had become a couple as had Sarah and Pete. Sarah failed with Adam and Megan, but Eve eventually became hers. Tara and Beth were inseparable. She wouldn't leave her side.

Marcos seemed to be content belonging to no one, however he was my constant shadow. I was more of a mentor than a father.

A few days after Maria's baby was born, she and Jorge came up to me, he put his hand on my shoulder. "Nick... Maria and I would be honored if you would join us at the baptism we're having in three days. We would like you and Beth to be the baby's godparents."

I hadn't had many religious friends. Beth frightened them all away. I wasn't sure what being a godparent entailed. "Well, I'll talk to Beth, but I've got to warn you, she's not all that big on religious traditions. I'll talk to her."

I could never get her to go to any symbolic ritual pertaining to any religion. She was a devout atheist. Her science was her religion. Everything could be explained by mathematics and physics. She believed that man created God. Until it was proven to her, she wasn't into "blind faith." I've never seen her pray, not even when we were looking for her son and grandchildren.

"What's the baby's name?" I asked.

Holding the baby to her breast, Maria answered. "We're not going to name him until his baptism. I want you to hold him when he is cleansed of his original sin. Jorge and I have seen enough baptisms we can do the service by heart. Even though a priest isn't going to be there, I know God will be beside us."

The firelight gave us a clear view of this new addition to our group as he suckled. Shame no longer existed. We were family. I was witnessing the beginning of the next generation: the first generation of the new world. As I watched I thought, why should mothers have hidden their breast when they fed their children? At what point did we as a civilization decide that breastfeeding was something that needs to be hidden? Adults eat in public, why can't our children? That was one thing we could change today.

I snapped out of deep thought again to answer Maria. "Yes I'm sure we would both be proud to be your child's godparents."

"Do you have any suggestions for names, Nick?" Maria asked.

"No." Naming babies wasn't one of my things. "I'll think about it, and I'll ask his godmother-to-be."

"Thank you, Nick." Jorge shook my hand, brandishing his signature smile.

"As long as you don't name him George, anything's okay," I said, smirking.

They both laughed then went back to adoring their new child.

I went over to Beth who was reading the remains of a magazine to Tara on the other side of the fire.

I tried to come up with a way to ask Beth about going to a baptism without wakening demons. If I could convince her that this was the happiest I'd seen anyone since the event took place, perhaps she'd consider their request. Jorge and Maria had everything to live for. They had a son to care for, and they had their God. How could that be so bad?

I intentionally interrupted Beth while she was reading. "They remind me of the Amish we had around our town; some of the happiest people I've ever met."

"Who's that?" Beth asked.

"Jorge and Maria. They remind me of the Amish. I wonder if they made it."

"They're right over there, what's wrong with you?" Her attention was split between Tara and me. Tara was getting more than her share, as usual.

"No, the Amish. I wonder if they made it. If they did, I'm sure they'll continue to survive. They were taught the old ways. They also taught their children discipline, religion, and how to work. What did we teach our children? Readin', writin' and 'rithmetic. Who taught their kids about finding water or catching rats? Nobody, that's who. Who taught our children? Society educated our children with contractors. Facts were memorized. Test results proved that the system worked. Survival skills and morals were not on the curriculum. Did we teach problem solving, survival skills, or even ethics?" I paused to take a breath or two. I hadn't planned to get as worked up as I had.

"What does religion have to do with the ability to survive?"

Now I had all of Beth's attention. "Well I've been talking to George and Maria. They're very religious you know."

"Yea...and...?" I could tell the old Beth was still around.

"They want us to be the baby's godparents." I paused before daring to speak again. "At the baby's baptism."

"Oh, so we're going to start that again. Why should we continue to believe in those old ancient myths and stories, when many of them have been proven to have been distorted and manipulated to control the population? Most of the bloodiest wars have been fought in the name of religion. Let's face it, we are just another species going extinct. There is no God!"

I knew I had opened up Pandora's Box. I was sure the others could hear, but I wasn't going to be overpowered by her this time. This time was different. Speaking one notch below yelling I said, "We've had these discussions before, and you know how I feel. Maria and Jorge are happy. Is that a bad thing? If their faith makes this place more bearable then so be it. That's their business. Tolerate it and move on. Not everybody believed what N.A.S.A said to be true all the time either. Looks to me like they dropped the ball on this one, didn't they?" I knew that, in her opinion, I had just blasphemed.

The crackling fire was the only sound, not even the children dared speak.

"Will you be there with me at the baby's baptism?"

"Might as well," she said with a sigh. "Science just took a ten-thousand-year backwards step. Baptism huh...? Is there going to be a witchdoctor with a bone through her nose?"

Beth went to the baptism and performed just as Maria and Jorge wanted her to. Beth and I promised to take care of Emanuel should anything happen to the both of them.

To celebrate we roasted a large beaver. Turning it on a spit over an open fire, the meal took on a luau type atmosphere.

Jorge and Maria led everyone in the Lord's Prayer. Everyone except Beth.

We each had gifts for the baby. Marcos scavenged until he found some cloth durable enough to be used as diapers. Pete and Sarah worked together to make a pack to carry the baby while we were between shelters. Pete gathered and dried the reeds, and Sarah wove them into a pack. Beth went to the baptism, and I felt I had given enough being the godfather.

Chapter 32
Mentoring a New Apprentice.

Beavers and opossums were our main source of food. We seldom needed to eat rats anymore. We continued to follow the swamps. By following the water, we came upon many culverts—too small for shelter, but excellent places to hang snares. Occasionally we would find one big enough to spend a night or two.

One time we stumbled across a railroad trestle made of old fashioned concrete, back when they still had railroads. As old as it was, it had withstood the earthquake.

Water ran through one side of the arched shelter, but the other side was high and dry. The wind was perfect so a fire could be built and the smoke would drift away from the sleeping area.

We still had a lot of supplies and could have kept moving for a couple of more days, but the trestle just said home, at least for a few days. We weren't heading anywhere fast anyways.

We set up camp. The girls started supper: more opossum stew.

Pete and Jorge were gathering railroad ties from the old tracks above. Buried in earth, the bottom half was unburned. The ties were easily found without a lot of walking. We decided that the two youngest men would tackle the duty of bringing them down the hill. Actually getting them down was the easy part. The hill was so steep, they would roll all the way to the bottom. The breeze blowing through would take out the thick smoke of the creosote-laden ties.

Getting to the top was easier for them than it was for me, so Marcos and I gathered our traps and started looking for signs of animals.

We weren't far from the others when I noticed a couple of freshwater clam shells near a pool. They didn't look like they had been there all that long and they were all opened.

First of all that meant there were clams out in deeper water that we could eat. We hadn't had any luck fishing. Clams and crayfish were all we'd been able to eat that came from the water. Even though I still had the fishing line, fishing was a waste of time. I spent a lot of valuable time waiting for a bite.

Secondly it meant that there was a raccoon nearby. I hadn't thought that any of them had survived, but apparently at least one had; and I knew how to catch him. I just hoped he wasn't the last of the species. I would hate to be known as the man who ate the last raccoon.

I instructed my young apprentice, "Marcos, take the torch and look for a trail next to the river's edge. The ground will be matted down along a path. You will see tracks in the mud at the water's edge." He could bend down better than I could.

"Are these some tracks?" Marcos asked, pointing to the mud.

"Tell me what they look like; I can't bend over 'cause my back is killing me." I could get a pill from Beth when I got back.

"They have five fingers and look like a little hand," he said, kneeling and bending with his head mere inches from the tracks.

"Do they look like they have a thumb?" I asked.

"No they look like they are all spaced about the same distance apart."

"No thumb on one, but not on the other?" I asked reassuring myself, and teaching Marcos the difference between a raccoon track and an opossum track.

"No, they're both about the same. What are they from, another possum?" He was intrigued by tracking. For a city boy, woodsmanship came easy.

"No, I think we have a coon living off these clams in this pool. Wanna catch him?"

"Can ya eat 'em? What do they look like?"

I couldn't believe he didn't know what a raccoon was. I loved to teach about wildlife. I used to take Beth up to the woods all the time. "Well, they're about the size of a fat cat or a small dog. They have black around their eyes. They look like a bandit, you know, a bank robber, a thief. And that's what they are. That's how you catch them. If they're around, put out a little food with a lot of smell, and you'll catch them. They like shiny things too. I used to place a piece of aluminum foil on the trap pan when I trapped. That's what we're going to do tonight. As for eating one, I never did, but a Native American fellow that I used to work with said they taste good but are greasy. I caught many when I was a trapper and can attest to the greasy part. When I used to skin them the fat was slimy. I was never hungry enough to eat one."

Although there wasn't any moonlight, I knew that any type of shiny metal would draw its attention. I showed Marcos how to set the trap at the end of the path that had been worn down. He placed a steel trap, one of many we found on somebody's garage floor, one half inch below the water's surface.

I had never used this type of set before because we had never encountered raccoons until now. They lived mostly in trees, and I was sure most of them perished.

Aluminum foil is what I used to use to wrap around the trap pan. The pan is where you would put the cheese on a mousetrap. It's a trigger. The aluminum foil would draw the raccoon's curiosity, he would reach out with his hand, and snap! We would have supper and maybe a coonskin hat for Marcos.

Any aluminum foil that we had was used so many times in the fire to cook that the entire luster had gone.

I needed something that would draw the attention of an animal with the keenest of senses, something that shined even in the dimmest light, something with flash.

There was only one thing I could think of. Beth was reluctant to give them up, but when I assured her that she would get them back, she loaned me her diamonds to use as bait.

I'd caught one cunning animal with them, so I figured I could catch another.

Chapter 33
Therapy

The two of us set enough traps to assure raccoon for supper tomorrow night.

Marcos filled his pockets with clams. We were getting very efficient at providing for ourselves. Every stream held something, every pond, every swamp. If there was an animal living nearby, we could catch it.

Pete and Jorge had brought down enough wood to last a week if needed. Supper was on the table. Well, we didn't have a table, but we did have bowls and spoons. Forks and plates weren't necessary because anything we ate either had a bone we could hold on to, or was made into stew. Plates would just be that much extra weight to carry when we were traveling around the swamps. No napkins, just our sleeves; those of us who had them.

Possum stew and freshwater clams made up the entrée. At one time I never would have eaten freshwater clams. They were too full of heavy metals to make them safe to eat, but now it was a short term goal to survive, not a long term one.

We all had full bellies and plenty of water.

The children were able to play around the wall on the dry slope of the riverbank. We could see them from a distance due to the size of the fire. It lit up the whole area and beyond. We loved the light, and there were plenty of railroad ties. There was sign up stream and we hadn't even checked down stream. All was good.

Marcos, Tara, and Eve were throwing stones into the water at the other end of the trestle. Beth was watching them like a hawk—no an owl. They see better in the dark.

Sarah and Pete were talking alone up by the entrance to the trestle.

Maria and Jorge were devoting all their attention to the new baby. When Maria wasn't nursing the baby she was busy making him a wrap made out of muskrat fur, it was the softest fur we had. The snows had ceased, but the nights were still cold, especially for an infant.

Beth and I were left alone for the first time since we found the other nurses and the children. The crying had stopped long ago and laughter took its place.

"Do you want to go wash up at that pond upstream you told us about?" Beth asked with a subtle tone in her voice that I thought had gone extinct with most everything else.

"We've got some traps set up there. Wanna explore downstream? I'll rig up a torch." I didn't want to disturb the area and ruin the trapping where Marcos had worked so hard. I wanted him to find something in the morning.

Pete and Sarah returned.

I liked to pick on Pete. He was so quiet for such a big man. "Where have you two been?" I asked, just to get a rise out of him.

"Sarah was just telling me about the trains that used to travel on the tracks." Pete looked down at Sarah and smiled. "She was telling me about the..."

Beth interrupted. "Sarah, can you watch the kids while we go look for more tracks?"

"Yea, we'll watch 'em," Sarah said with her usual snotty tone of voice. She only talked to Beth that way. She was slowly becoming tolerant of everyone else.

We walked away holding hands, until Beth turned and said, "Don't let them out of your sight!"

"Let's go, Beth!" I yanked her by the hand before she could ruin the moment with a confrontation. "Thanks, Sarah. We won't be gone long."

"We better be." She jumped up to whisper in my ear. When she came back down she grabbed my ass—the first time since her grandbabies died.

We walked along the riverbank until the light from the tunnel could no longer be seen. That's when Beth took the torch from my hand and stuck it in the stream, drowning its light.

"Guess, it's going to be harder to find tracks now, isn't it?" In the second after the words were out of my mouth, Beth's tongue was in it.

All the emotions suppressed due to the conditions of the past ten months surfaced on that sandy bank.

The last time I'd been with Beth, she was a third heavier. I was seeing Beth as she was twenty years ago. This was the first I noticed.

The aches and pains that accompanied both of us disappeared briefly as adrenalin substituted for Oxycodone.

This was the therapy we both needed.

"Well nurse... I think...I'm cured!" Breathlessly, I looked up at her. There wasn't enough light to make out the color of her hair. I knew it was grey, but in the dark, it was red again. It had grown back.

"You're the patient...I'm the nurse... I'll tell you...when you're cured.... You need some more... sessions," she said as she collapsed and lay on the sand.

The love we made that night had more passion than the first night we spent in the camper, or any time in-between, and this time she was sober.

Once we both caught our breath, we shook the sand out of our clothes and went back to the others. Our torch was out.

Beth found it romantic that we walked arm in arm back to the others, but it was due to my weakened legs that the trip back took longer. I'll never tell her that.

"Where did you guys go?" Marcos said. Our arrival distracted him from a drawing he was scratching on the concrete walls of the trestle.

"We just went down stream to look for more signs of wildlife. Uh... then our torch went out," I said.

"Did you find any? Are there more coon tracks? You told me that I was going to help you do more scouting. You're going to take me tomorrow, aren't you, Nick?"

"You bet. I know you'll have something," I said in an attempt to stymie his curiosity of our whereabouts.

"What are you drawing?" Beth asked, having the same goal.

"It's Mommy." He had never talked about his mother when we asked what happened to her.

Beth placed the torch into the fire to ignite the oil-soaked fibers and held it closer to the drawing. Only when the wind blew steadily, carrying away the smoke, could the full image be seen all at once.

He had scratched a picture of a woman with her clothes and hair on fire. The picture was within a circle, except for the arms. The arms extended out of the circle as if hanging down. The mouth of the woman was open wide as if screaming out in pain.

"Was that the last time you saw your mom, Marcos?" I asked.

"This is when she put me under the road, in that hole that they were working in. She put me in and then dropped me. I fell to the bottom and couldn't get back up to Mommy to help her. Fire, and sparks, and smoke was coming in the hole, then she was gone. After that I had to run down into the dark, it was burning me. There was two other guys down there. They had white hardhats. I think they died when it was so hard to breath." His demeanor had turned quite somber.

Beth placed her arm around his shoulder. "Hey, Marcos, Nick says you're pretty good at setting traps and should have us a coon for supper tomorrow."

Instantaneously his expression changed from one that was about to develop tears, into a full-blown smile. The only other smile I have seen bigger was that of Jorge when Maria's baby was born.

Chapter 34
The Wall

The whole side of the wall of the trestle was covered with artwork, but only up to about four feet. Most of it was indistinguishable scribbles. Marcos' drawings could be identified. There was the one of his mom. There was one of a campfire surrounded by the exact number of people in our group. My favorite was one of him with his first coon. He spent a great deal of time insuring the coon was as close to the real thing as he could. He did a good job.

Beth and I were looking at the newest renaissance when she inquired, "What would you draw?"

I thought for a while, then I said, "A deer, I guess. I don't know."

"You can't draw a deer."

Of course I couldn't. "Why not? I'm the artist. I can draw anything I want."

"It would be like drawing a dinosaur. They don't exist in our world. This wall could be a message to other survivors. If we draw deer, they might think we found some. We should draw pictures of animals that still exist, the ones that we are living on, and instructions on how to catch them. Let's make this place a library of the most important facts of our time, so others might have a better chance."

Before we left, that shelter was covered on both sides with drawings, tips on how to survive, and lots of examples of how it used to be.

The remaining space belonged to the adults. Extra torches were put about until the whole trestle was lit up. We became obsessed with the project. We eventually erected scaffolding made from piled up railroad ties to extend our reach higher.

I illustrated how to make deadfalls, and snares for those who didn't have leg traps like we did. I went into detail about the process of skinning and butchering. I contributed survival tips.

Beth, Sarah, and Maria worked together on first aid tips, and basic life saving techniques.

Maria wrote down recipes for all the things we have been eating. She scratched several prayers into the area surrounding a very life like portrait of Emanuel and herself.

The portrait was Jorge's contribution. "I like it, but I wish I had a way to add color. Your beautiful brown hair and eyes look black. I want to show what you look like in the sunshine."

Sarah sat up bumping Pete's big nose as she rose. "We can get you some paint, Jorge." She stood up and headed for the stream. Unsure of her footing on the rocky riverbed, she carefully looked at the rocks, torch to the ground. She would pick one up, look at it, and either toss it back in the river or put it in one of her pockets.

When she returned she took some of the raccoon fat that we used to grease our boots to make them more waterproof, and put it in a pot to render it down. The smell gagged any of us who were unfortunate enough to be down wind. While the fat was slowly heating, Sarah began crushing white, brown, red and black pebbles between two flat stones. She kept each type of rock in a separate pile consisting of now, only dust. She took the fat, rendered down to liquid, and mixed it with the powered stones, a little at a time until the dust took the appearance of four separate colors of paint on an artist pallet.

"Here you go Jorge, here's your paint." Sarah handed the flat stone to Jorge. "You'll have to find something for a brush."

Jorge accepted the gift. His smile said thank you for him.

"Come here girls." Both toddlers ran up to Sarah. "Put your hands up to the wall and I'll paint you."

The children and Marcos put their hands up against the wall as if they were being frisked. Sarah held one hand from each while she blew the remaining dust from the stones against their little fingers. After each pulled away, the silhouette of a hand remained on the side of the wall.

"How did you know how to do that?" Beth asked.

"I had other aspirations in college, but as you know, nursing paid the bills." This was the first cordial answer Beth had ever received from Sarah.

Pete added nothing to the wall. He forfeited his share to Sarah and spent his time building scaffolding, then tearing it down to rebuild it again.

The apparent truce between Beth and Sarah was short-lived. Sarah started using more than her share of space to write down the history of the world up to the point that things went to hell.

This caused things to go to hell here. Beth could take no more. "You don't have to write so big. You've taken up enough of the wall as it is."

Sarah stopped writing and turned to give Beth one hell of a glare. "This is important historical information. There may be no records left. This might be a last chance to preserve history. That's more important than the planets or that junk you're writing about anyways. Nobody cares about that shit."

This was a blatant frontal attack on Beth's religion. She retaliated. "Just what is so important about the history of the human species? That he existed?"

"We need to study history so we won't repeat the same mistakes," Sarah argued.

"We had the chance to study history and learn from it but we didn't," Beth responded.

"What do mean?" Sarah asked, with a more reserved tone, she was trying to think what part of human history Beth was talking about.

"We knew what happened to the dinosaurs, but we had a, 'That will never happen to us,' attitude. Our arrogance, and faith in our technology, caused us to neglect the possibility that this could happen. We learned from our history, but not the planet's. If more people would have concentrated on science, this may have been prevented." She was trying her best to defend her need to put down her passion on the wall too. "Plus, that's all your writing is about, the human history. If there isn't something left about science, then any other people finding it ... " reasoning temporarily escaped her. "They still need to know...." Tears streamed down her face. "Maybe it doesn't matter." She was growing tired of arguing with Sarah. This wasn't the Beth I used to know. She would never have given up her faith this quickly before.

"Okay, okay. We'll split Pete's share." Sarah mellowed knowing her victory was bittersweet. A half of Pete's share was her way of saying sorry.

Beth was happy with the extra space to record her science. They both started writing smaller, just to fit as much material on the wall as possible. This might be one of our last chances to rerecord history. We had to let somebody know what had been.

Nobody suspected that Sarah was so knowledgeable when it came to history. She had been a history major before she had taken up nursing. Her addition to the wall seemed more important to me than some of the science stuff that Beth contributed, but I would never say that out loud.

Chapter 35
An Atlatl

Just as they did with Emanuel's baptism, Jorge and Maria officiated at their own wedding. This too was recorded on the wall. Freshwater clams and raccoon was the feast served. No flowers, no priest, no rice, just witnesses. That was good enough. Their vows were accepted as truth by all present. Done deal.

This was one of those days. Everyone had enough food and water, the chores were done. We lay around watching the children play. Made me wonder why so many children were neglected in the past. They provided more entertainment than anything that once had been beamed around the planet.

Without warning one of the girls would get up and add one more thing to the last bit of space remaining on the wall.

Tara and Eve were playing with the empty clamshells. They would throw them against the wall to watch them break, a trick they learned from Marcos. They didn't have the strength to break many, but when they did it was a major accomplishment followed by great celebration on their part: dancing and laughing and jumping around.

Beth and I were lying on some of the larger pelts up against the wall away from the breeze. Our spot was nearest the fire. Seniority had its privileges.

Maria came walking over to us. "Nick you haven't held your godchild in a while." She forced the baby into my arms. "Beth holds him all the time. Don't you love little Manny?"

Doing my best not to have his head break off in my hands, I held Jorge's son. "Oh... he's nice." What an idiot. "Of course I love him. I'm just not much of a baby person." I handed Manny back and stood up to throw more railroad ties on the fire. Occasionally the wind would shift and blow the smoke directly at us, but we found that if we kept a hot fire, more smoke would be burned off.

Dejected, Maria handed the boy to Beth, who gladly accepted. "What's wrong, was that miserable old man mean to my baby?" She held him up and kissed him repeatedly. "Ninny will take care of him later. I think he needs another stress session, old grump." She laid the baby down to check the diaper that had once served as a shirt to some factory worker named Evans.

Marcos was throwing a stick at a ledge along the edge of the river. He placed an old soda can on the sandy bank. He only hit the can a couple of times, and then with the side of the stick as it hit the hill sideways. The can would tumble into the water, only to be retrieved again and set up for another try. We all enjoyed his antics.

Around his neck dangled a new trophy. The raccoon he harvested was a boar. Few people know it, but the male raccoon has a bone in its penis. I thought it would make a nice trophy for him, dangling from a beaver leather string. Every time he caught a boar, he could add to his necklace. The women were disgusted with the idea. No matter how much they voiced their opinions, the necklace stayed. Of course I took the brunt of the tongue lashings.

Sarah put her hand on Pete's leg and said, "Pete, go get me one of those trees that Marcos made that spear out of. One only about one inch around, but bring me roots and all."

"What do you want that for?" Pete asked.

"Just get me one with a one inch base and lots of roots. I'll show you when you get back." This was an order, not a request.

Poor Pete. He really didn't have much to choose from. There were no more fish in the sea.

Pete was only gone about five minutes when he returned soaked from the waist down, with her tree, roots and all.

Sarah inspected the tree to see how the roots were formed. "That should do just fine. Now cut off the roots about seven or eight inches from the bottom and we'll make him another spear."

"Then what did you want the roots for?" Pete asked in a disgusted tone. He wouldn't have gone in the water if not for the roots.

"You'll see. Give me your knife." No please or thank you ever came from Sarah's mouth.

Once Pete handed her the roots and the knife she started to hollow out a bend in the base, where the roots met the trunk. After about a half hour or so of concentrated digging, she had made a hole into the roots a little bigger than the diameter of Marcos' spear. "Marcos, bring your stick over here. I made you something, but put that can back up first," Sarah yelled.

He placed his target back up on the hill, supporting the bottom with rocks. When the can would stay in place, he turned and came splashing over to Sarah.

"Did you see me hit it? Nick, do you think I could kill a raccoon with this?" he asked as he handed his weapon to Sarah.

"You might scare one away," I said.

"You'll be able to when you practice more," Sarah said as she placed the end of his spear into the hole she carved. Then she laid down the spear and carved a little more at the roots. Now the hole was the size she wanted. What she had made was a device to put the end of his spear into before he threw it.

"Hold this and your spear like this," she demonstrated how to hold the new invention, handle and spear in line with one another, spear resting in the hollowed out end. "This is called an Atlatl. Early man used to use them to hunt small animals."

This caught Beth's attention. "Some believe this invention is what gave Homo sapiens the advantage over Neanderthals long ago. Isn't that right?"

"This handle will make it so you can throw farther and more accurately." Sarah's lack of response seemed out of place since they both worked so hard on the wall together. "There's no reason you couldn't kill something if you get good enough with it. Just hold it like this; hold on to the handle and let go of the spear when you throw." She looked at Beth and said, "Yeah, that's what they say."

As Marcos practiced, Beth and Sarah watched. The overlapping of history and science was the only thing that these two nurses could find to talk about. Once they started talking the rest of us couldn't get a word in.

It took a while but Marcos killed that can several times while we were there.

Chapter 36
More Instruction

The time spent at the trestle turned out to be our happiest. Leaving reminded me of the last day of a vacation when you packed suitcases before an early flight; we didn't want to go, but knew we had to. The food at the trestle had all been harvested. There was no reason to stay.

Days and weeks were finally measurable. The light shown through the clouds barely enough to distinguish day from night. Our sleep patterns returned to normal, and our moods improved as well. Sadly, sunshine still couldn't poke its way through the thick cover for longer than a minute or two a week, but when it did, all eyes looked up.

One time while our group stopped to make a fire, the sun came out. The thickest clouds parted without warning and the star's rays warmed everyone the instant it touched our faces. Like Aztecs, we all worshiped the sun from the moment it showed blinding light on our dismal surroundings.

The women stripped every child and held each of them up over their heads. Jorge held little Manny over his head, he was taller than Maria.

"What to hell are they doing?" I asked Pete.

"I don't know, something about crickets," he said.

Sarah laughed. "Rickets, not crickets, you big dummy. The children are lacking vitamin D. Sunshine is good for them, and without it they could get rickets." She laughed again. "Crickets."

Beth turned while still holding naked Tara. "I want you to save the livers from anything you catch from now on too. We'll give them to the kids. That's another way they can get vitamin D."

Like someone who suffered from seasonal stress disorder, I could feel my demeanor improve as the rays warmed my face.

All too soon it turned dark again, the children were dressed, and we went back to our nocturnal ways. Once again, the fire was our only source of light.

We were staying next to a wall with a makeshift roof that Pete and I had constructed with the fur tarp.

Travelling from swamp to swamp left us without fresh meat the first day in a new shelter. We found that it was better to send at least one of the party ahead to find shelter or swamps showing good signs of life. He would set traps, gather wood to get the fire started, and then return to lead the rest.

Jorge drew the short straw. I was leery about sending him out alone. "Make sure you mark your route so you can find your way back to us. We'll have supper on when you get back."

Kissing his family goodbye, he took five of the leg-hold traps and a canteen of water, and trudged off into the dark.

I knew that Jorge would be back in two days. I had a promise to keep. Time to earn my keep. Before I went out to check my traps I threw some more wood on the fire. Marcos gathered enough to keep the area warm and lit all day while we were gone. We would get some more while we were checking traps. It seemed we'd been bringing home more wood than meat for about two weeks. Pickings had been hard since we left the trestle.

I threw one last log on the fire before waking Beth. I kissed her, and then whispered so as not to wake the others, "We'll be back with supper."

She looked up at me with Tara still asleep in her arms, gave me one of those looks of desperation that tears my heart out, then smiled and said, "Be careful. I love you."

Her goodbye seemed more solemn than normal. "Don't worry, hon. We're going to make it," I said, as I combed my fingers through her hair. "I think the sun's poking through more and more each day."

The fire lit up the shelter as Marcos and I left for the swamp. I had done this so many times I knew every stream, stump, and stone by heart. Using a torch wasn't necessary, I just had to follow the water and I'd come on to my traps.

One by one, empty trap after empty trap, the morning went on. One trap had caught something, but it had pulled away. We needed to cut some teeth in the jaws so the animal's chance of getting away decreased. When I had trapped before, the laws stated that traps could not have teeth. There was no law now. Our conscience was our guide. Feeding all of us was what was important. We needed a hacksaw. We'd left one behind when we abandoned the fork truck, but we could only carry so much.

"Trap number eleven should be just down here," I told Marcos. I strained to see in the darkness, looking for a stick standing upright in the mud with a white ribbon tied to the end. I took a few more steps to find my exact location. I realized I'd gone too far. Had I missed it or had it been set?

"Here it is Nick...I think," Marcos yelled excitedly, but without conviction.

I reached for my Bic lighter. It had long since run out of fuel but the sparker still worked. When I flicked it a couple of times I noticed my flag was laying in the water.

The feeling I got then, was that of a parent on Christmas morning, when there were Christmas mornings. Marcos was as excited as he would be with a new toy wrapped in shiny gold paper.

That stick hadn't fallen down by itself, and he knew it. I had tied some wire to a log; the end of the wire held a fishhook baited with the guts of a muskrat. The log had been pulled out towards the pond, but got hung up on the rocks Marcos strategically placed.

I waded out into the water, reached down, and fished in the dark for the wire. I wanted Marcos to learn, but he wasn't ready for this quite yet. "I could lose a finger this way, you know." We both laughed remembering the beaver incident. Finding the wire, I started pulling, hoping to feel something pull back. As I pulled, I felt tension. I backed away from the shore and handed the wire to Marcos.

He walked backwards higher onto the bank, slipping and falling twice.

I was cautiously waiting for what I knew was on the other end. Our catch's unique shape broke above the water line. "Dinner!" I pulled the snapper onto dry land. Now I could keep my promise to Jorge. As I attended to the reptile, I instructed, "Just pull the wire until you hear the hiss, then carefully put your foot down and hold the shell down till you can find the head. Hold the wire taunt to keep the head out." I struggled to pull the head all the way out to keep my fingers away from its jaws. I started to saw. The thick skin of the reptile's neck was as tough as leather. When I got to the spine I had to twist the blade to get between the vertebrae. A crunching sound told me that I had easy cutting from there on. "Then slice around the shell until the hissing stops." Surprising how fast you develop standard operating procedures after you lose a finger to an animal in the dark.

I rebaited the hooks with the head and moved on to my next trap. Marcos was happy to carry the fifteen-pound plus turtle. One wasn't enough to feed everyone, but it would make the rations go further. She was a big female and might have eggs in her.

The rest of the traps were empty. No big surprise. I picked up some wood for the fire and dragged it back to the shelter. Marcos was having all he could do to carry the turtle.

The light of the fire led us home. Beth's somber face was the first thing we saw. The freckles said, "redhead," even though her hair hadn't since it grew back.

Marcos dangled the turtle in the air while he ran the last few yards, as if he had won some award. "Look, look what we got. I found it, Nick walked right by it."

She tried to eke out a smile, and finally did, but I knew it wasn't for the turtle. Usually she would praise us for our success. Something else was bothering her.

Chapter 37
Grit

The two days went by fast. "Nick, Nick," I heard him calling. I could see his smile long before I could understand his shouts. Jorge returned with a surprise: another person.

From a distance the stranger reminded me of that Tex fellow, though I had taken care of him permanently. I immediately went on the defensive, as did Pete.

We'd ditched the gun long ago. Looking for ammunition was the problem. Gunpowder and fire didn't mix. I wasn't too worried with Pete here. Even though our diet had been far less calorie intake than I'm sure Pete was used to, he was still a big man, with a fist about the size of a softball.

We were both scoping out the newcomer. At first glance the stranger looked larger than Jorge, but several layers of clothing gave the illusion of bulk. Once we saw his hands and face it was clear he was thinner than Jorge who went one hundred fifty when his belly was full.

"Nick, Nick... look I found somebody alive." Jorge looked happy, but then he always did. "Nick, this is Grit. I found him while I was at our new spot. Grit hasn't even been trapping, just looking in cellars." Jorge was so proud of himself.

"Hi, Grit." I waited for a response, but the toothpick of a man remained silent. "Tell us about yourself and what you've been eating and what you've seen. My name's Nick and this is Pete, obviously you've met Jorge. We don't have much food to offer you but we will have some soup ready soon. Keep ya' going for a couple of days." I felt like Mick, now rationing out the food, with those in our party coming first.

Jorge said, "He's been living off canned food that he found in cellars, and that's all. All he has is a knife, a spoon, and a can opener. Can you believe that?"

"Why don't you let him speak for himself?" I wanted to feel this guy out.

"Hey..., they call me Grit. I come from Louisiana. It's all gone."

I shook his hand, wiped his sweat on my pant leg, and asked, "Are you all alone?"

"I've always been alone."

"Well come eat and we can talk." Our last two additions had contributed to our group, and I could see no reason why another mouth to feed would hamper our progress. It would lessen the workload on the rest of us.

We offered him the broth and a couple pieces of jerky; we could spare no more.

He ate without speaking. He tilted the bowl and drank without using the spoon. The soup was very hot. His first mouthful spilled out from his lips. He continued to chug, spilling half. The noises he made resembled a dog eating.

When he finished, I asked again, "So how have you been living all alone?"

"House to house. There's always some cans if you look hard enough." His beard held another five percent of his supper. "I found a turtle once; fucker bit me so I smashed it on the road till I killed it." With nothing more to eat, our guest began surveying the surroundings. He looked around in jerky movements. Staring at each of us individually, making everyone equally nervous.

Grit began glaring at the women. "Who's this?" he asked, putting me back on full alert. Although leery of his inquisitiveness, I began to introduce everyone, pointing to each. "This is my wife Beth, and Tara. This is Sarah and Eve. This is Maria and Emanuel. This is Marcos," I said as I rubbed the young boy's head. "You've already met Jorge and Pete." I changed the subject to distract him from the women. "Have you seen any area that hasn't been burned, or maybe burned less?"

"No," he said. "No..." He started to choke and gasp for air. This went on for a minute or so before he could answer clearly. "No, it's all the same everywhere. What wasn't flooded in Louisiana burned." Grit was looking at one of the torches we'd made, as he continued to cough and hack, spitting repeatedly. "This is the first light I've seen except for the few times that the sun came out, or lightning."

"You mean you haven't even been keeping fires? How did you stay warm when it was cold?" Sarah asked.

"I've been cold a lot!" he said. "I stayed in a big boat about five miles from the ocean. Again he coughed and spit up a disgusting bunch of bile. "I stayed there for about six months. I still feel like I'm walking sideways."

"Is there any organization at all anywhere?" Beth asked.

"Every time I went into a city, they tried to kill me. People from small towns moved to the cities. The food ran out early. Every city I've been to has animals there now, and I don't mean the ones with four legs. You can't deal with 'em. All they want to do is boss you around, threaten you. Don't care what you think 'bout your life. You mean food to them. Lotta killin', lotta just plain dying. These houses in the country haven't been picked over." He picked his nose. "Where can I get some sleep?"

Surprised at his abruptness I answered, "Yea...um... you can sleep over there next to the wall, near that old tank, if you want to.

He shuffled over to the tank, cleaned a clear spot on the blackened cement and, without something to soften his bed, or for under his head, he lay down, not to speak again.

Chapter 38
Wrong Turns

While he was sleeping we discussed whether we should accept another into our group. We all felt that we must. Though strange, Grit was a human too, and he could contribute his share of work.

In the morning we woke to a sky brighter than any so far, though still darker than twilight. Grit was slow to get moving, but eventually followed us. Jorge took the lead to the new shelter he'd found. Soon it was obvious that he was lost. In the excitement of finding Grit, he failed to mark his back trail. Grit was no help at all. His suggestions only made Jorge more confused.

Now we were scouting as we went. Jorge's two days of preparation might as well not have happened. The five traps he set in the new location were lost.

We all walked along a riverbank, taking breaks when feeder streams would appear. The group would sit and wait for one of the men to explore the narrow waterway. That was where the swamps would be found. The whole exploratory process usually took an hour or so. If there was nothing promising found, then we'd move up river a little farther.

This waiting time was usually spent building a fire, and supper would be ready for the return of the scout. Only this time we didn't have anything to eat.

It was Pete's turn to take the long walk upstream.

Marcos and I were looking for crayfish under rocks in the river to no avail. We finally conceded and started looking for turtles on the banks, with the same results.

The wait for Pete's return this time was longer than usual. We started to worry about him. Pete was no wimp; he could take care of himself. Something must have happened. Did he fall and break a leg, have a heart attack, or become the victim of some unimaginable fate? We decided to wait a little longer, and if there was still no sign, then Jorge and I would venture off to find him. It would be easy to track him along the water's edge amidst the muddy banks.

I was very apprehensive about leaving Grit alone with the rest. I hadn't had much chance to get to know him. He was very quiet, and hadn't given much in the way of anything, including his share of the work. He was content to sit by the fire and watch everyone else give more than their share.

I needed Jorge. We knew how the other worked. We could search two directions at the same time, and if we lost the trail we could find each other again. Marcos wouldn't have been much help if we had to carry Pete back. He was still just a kid.

I kissed Beth. "Wait here until we come back. We'll be back with him. I guarantee it," I assured Sarah.

Beth's grasp on my arm tightened. "I should be going with you, Nick. What if he needs medical attention?"

She was right. And one more to carry him would be better.

"Grit, we're going to find Pete," I said. "You stay here with everyone else and don't do anything!"

Beth mumbled under breath, "That's what he's good at."

"Don't bother looking for food or anything, just keep the group together right here. Especially Marcos, he'll want to wander off and look for tracks. We'll be back before you know it."

The features in Grit's face became clearer and more pockmarked than I had imagined. The sun had come out.

All talking ceased and we just stared at the sun, shielding our eyes from its beautiful brilliance. It stayed out for about a minute. Its brief but powerful performances were always announced by a standing ovation accompanied with generous amounts of cheering and clapping. Then it would go in again. Only to be followed by immediate silence and depression.

Once the show was over, it was as if it never happened. "Well let's go get him," I said.

Walking upstream, Marcos met me to say good-bye. I whispered, "Watch that Grit guy. Keep everyone safe. And don't wander off. Keep in sight, okay? We'll be back soon."

"Okay, Nick. Can I get a torch and look for tracks?" he asked with hope in his voice.

"No, I told you to keep close to the others and watch the new guy."

"Okay, Nick." I could tell he was bored already, but I felt that I could count on him more than Grit.

Beth, Jorge and I left our group with a great deal of apprehension.

Following Pete's tracks could have been accomplished by Marcos with one eye shut. He left a deep track.

Walking became effortless when the river bottom turned to flat rock. Unfortunately this ease of walking was the reason that Pete took the same route. We had lost his track.

Jorge and I searched each side of the river. Beth walked down the middle with the torch. Neither I, nor Jorge could see well enough to be sure we hadn't missed a footprint.

"How much farther are we going to go? We could have walked by him." Beth was worried about him being injured.

"We're going to keep going upstream as long as this rock continues. When we get to the end of it we should find his tracks where he climbed out of the water." I wasn't so sure that we would find his track again. He could have turned off anywhere, and we could have missed it.

We continued upstream until we came upon another stream feeding the one we were in. We searched around the sandy bank for his prints but came up empty. We moved on upstream to another brook, not five hundred yards past the first.

"There!" We all said simultaneously. The indentations made by his enormous heel were unmistakable.

We followed his tracks for what seemed miles. His strides were two of mine and three of Beth's. We persevered, when suddenly it appeared that Pete headed off into the woods, or what was left of it.

His tracks were again simple to follow. The ground had nothing but a crusty layer of burnt dead moss.

I couldn't understand why Pete would leave the water. It was the only way back to our party since we didn't have a compass, and there were no road signs to point the way.

Our torch was getting low and we hadn't brought material to make another.

Finally we came back to the river where the water passed over the flat rock.

"He's headed back home, he's okay." We were overjoyed at the discovery. We hastened our pace, still being as cautious as possible. We didn't need to have Pete carry one of us out on a rescue mission.

We finally reached the main river and immediately headed over to the fire.

Seeing our torch Pete ran over to greet us. "Nick, I'm sorry I got lost. I thought I could go down and catch the other stream, but I got turned around." He threw up his hands. "Never mind that. We've got other problems."

Chapter 39
The Chase

I instinctively surveyed the area around the fire and did a head count. One was missing. "Grit!"

"Yep, he was the scum that we thought he was," Pete said.

"What did he do?" I asked, preparing myself for the worse. We didn't need this shit.

"He attacked Maria when she was breast feeding Emanuel. The baby's fine, so's Maria..." before he could continue the rest of his briefing, Jorge busted past both Pete and me, knocking Pete to the ground.

"Maria! Maria!" Weeping as he ran, the rest of his words were inaudible.

"Where is the scrawny bastard?" I wondered how to hell we'd deal with this. We had no laws, no rules. This was the first reason we had to need them.

Pete gave what I thought was a little laugh. "You want to hear the best part?"

I waited for him to go on without answering the rhetorical question, but he didn't. "What?" I said impatiently.

"Marcos caught him when he first started assaulting Maria, took out his little spear, and stuck it right in him. Hit him first time. The weirdo ran off upstream and hasn't come back." Pete was still kind of laughing.

"Did he rape her or what? Is she okay?" I was getting pissed at his lack of sensitivity.

"Oh, she's fine. She said he still had all his clothes on." Again it was obvious that Pete didn't see the severity of the situation.

"Where's Marcos?"

"He's over by the girls watching the other two kids. He wanted to go track that asshole, but Sarah wouldn't let him. She can be a hard ass sometimes, ya' know?" He laughed again.

"So now our biggest problem isn't that we don't have a shelter prepared for the night. It's not that we have no food. It's that we have a wounded dirt bag upstream, along the path that we planned to take."

Once Maria calmed down, we discussed our options as a group. We all felt that he was a danger, but we had to stay on our course, the river would lead us to food.

We decided to keep to our plan and follow the water. If we did confront him again, Pete, Jorge and I would deal with him. As much as Marcos wanted to, he was still just a boy.

We had no shelter and no food, and there was danger ahead, but we trudged through the dark. We came upon the same bedrock in the river that we had found while looking for Pete. Walking on the flat stone beneath our feet was a welcome respite from the constant danger of twisting an ankle on the slippery rocks.

The flat rock seemed to go on forever. We walked in the ankle deep water, as tepid as a summer's rain coming down the rain gutters during a hot afternoon's cloudburst. It was quiet except for the constant sound of insects, to which we became desensitized. All the children were sleeping in the knapsacks that Maria had crafted. Marcos followed behind Pete, Jorge, and me. He was looking for Grit's tracks. He carried his own torch, with his nose down to the ground, like a bloodhound on a hot trail.

We traveled in this formation for hours, silent, stopping when one of our group needed a rest. Everyone called a rest stop at one time or the other, except for Marcos.

At one of our more frequent rest stops Marcos cried out, "What's this? Nick, come here. There's something on this root." The excitement in his voice made me think it was more than a muskrat track.

Pete, Jorge, and I ran over to the riverbank to where Marcos was kneeling. "What did you find?"

"It's got blood on it." Marcos said as he poked at something with his other spear.

"Don't touch it!" Beth yelled out, running behind.

Pete and Jorge got to the bank sooner than I did. They took the tracking pose and knelt down to investigate Marcos' find.

"He hit him harder than we thought. That little thing packs a wallop." Again Pete had a tone to his voice that pointed more to jocularity than to the seriousness the situation deserved.

I had to look twice because of the poor light. I took Marcos' spear and reached out to poke at the find myself. Once I moved the object, it became clear that it was a piece of intestine. It had to have come from Grit. Marcos' spear had hit him hard enough to eviscerate him to the point that the bowels were catching on roots as he crawled along the riverbank. My past hunting experiences told me we would find him dead within a day.

Marcos continued his tracking duties. We found very little blood after we found the guts, a couple of more drops but then it ran out. We weren't sure if he had crawled onto the land and died, or maybe we walked right by his body. We gave up looking for him or fearing that he might show up. I was sure he was dead somewhere.

Pete couldn't let it go. "Well, I guess Nick will have to let you vote along with the rest of us now that you're a man, hey Marcos?"

"Is that true, Nick? Am I a man now, Nick?" His apparent need for my approval would have been uncomfortable to me in days gone past. Now it was something I cherished and I felt that I could finally teach a youngster something he would use and listen to. All the advice I had given every teenager before, when they had all the advantages of civilized life, had been wasted. Not one of them listened, or those that did, refused to heed it. I did have an unfair advantage on this one. If he didn't listen, he wouldn't live very long, though he was doing quite well so far.

Circumnavigating slow-moving water we came upon one of Grit's jackets. It was ripped and covered with blood.

"Marcos' atlatl couldn't do this," Beth said holding up the bloody garment.

Chapter 40
Predators

After several days our worries about coming across Grit diminished. We felt safe sending a scout ahead to find shelter, as long as he marked his trail so we didn't lose anyone again.

Jorge led us to a horse trailer only twenty feet from a slow moving river. The roof was intact and the windows could be covered with pelts to keep the wind out. The nights spent in the trailer would be cramped with all of us in there at the same time, but we'd grown accustomed to sleeping huddled together A small beach along the river would make a nice place for the children to play. Cattail stubs lined the small bay on each side.

While gathering the roots, Beth found a small stream feeding the river. "There's a creek just over the hill. The water is moving pretty fast over gravel. I tasted it and I think it should be okay as it is."

Normally we'd boil the water before we filled the containers, but Beth's judgment was seldom questioned. We filled the empty canteens with unpurified water, and settled in for the night.

I was jarred out of sleep by the sound of Beth throwing up outside the trailer. The water wasn't as good as she'd predicted. I got up, careful not to wake the rest. "Guess who's got beaver fever now!"

She heaved again, even louder than the previous round.

"Do you have the diarrhea yet?" I asked—a bit of revenge disguised as an attempt to prove I cared. My attempt at humor was poorly timed.

Just before her next episode she managed to force out, "Shut up!" The poor girl started to puke again. The guttural sounds were loud enough to wake the others.

She looked up with drool running down her chin. "It's not beaver fever, dumb ass." Now she started with dry heaves. Nothing came out.

I waited till the worst was over to speak. "Sure it is. You've got the same symptoms I had. I don't need to be a nurse to figure that out. Wait till the diarrhea kicks in." A hand touched my shoulder. I turned to see Sarah.

"Nick, it's not beaver fever. She's pregnant."

I looked at Beth who was looking up at me with spittle dripping.

"You can't be," I said. "You have that implant. You'll be fine in a couple of days. Dump out the canteens. Boil the hell out of that water and the canteens too. Make sure you drink a lot of good water today."

"It's not the water, Nick." Maria said, as she touched my other shoulder, confirming Sarah's statement.

"I thought you were too old for this anymore."

Another hand caressed the back of my head. It was Pete. "We've been able to find enough to eat so far. She can breast feed like Maria. Things will work out."

I did a double take to make sure who I was looking at. No matter how I looked at it, I couldn't change what was, but still couldn't believe it. Everyone knew about Beth's pregnancy before I did. I guess she wanted to practice or get advice about how to tell me. I had been left out of the loop.

All the women in the group were ecstatic about the news. Beth and Sarah were more sociable towards each other. The women already started coming up with names for the baby. Maria's suggestions all had some Christian connotations, like George, after St. George, slayer of the dragon. Sarah's suggestions all had some philosophical meaning to them, like Phoenix, for a boy, or Anastasia, for a girl.

I sat on the bank, watching the children playing on the beach, as I tried to digest the news.

Jorge came over and sat down next to me. "They really are a lot of fun, Nick. You never had kids of your own, did you?"

I rested my forearms on my knees. "No. Beth's kids were the only ones I've ever been around."

"You seem to be doing a good job with him." Jorge pointed to Marcos wading along the river's edge.

"I haven't done anything special. He's the one who hangs around me."

We watched him digging.

Marcos made sure we never ran out of roots. He waded in the rivers and swamps so much, his feet were permanently wrinkled. Even though we didn't always have meat, he always provided some sort of root, once I showed him how to recognize them. He yelled to me. "Hey, Nick, come look at these tracks!"

I stood up and walked along the bank.

"You'll be a good dad," Jorge said.

Looking back all I could see was his smile. Tara and Eve climbed on his back. I watched awhile. Jorge sure made being around kids look easy.

"Nick, really. These tracks are different than the others," Marcos yelled.

"Okay, I'm coming." I followed the bank up to the boy.

Holding up the torch so I could see, he pointed down. "See? These are big. Looks like it's dragging a tail like muskrats do, but way bigger."

I bent down to get a closer look when I heard a splash. Thinking one of the little ones had fallen in, I looked back at Jorge. A dark shadow lunged for one of the children.

Jorge pushed the toddler away and put his hands out to protect it. A five-foot alligator snapped onto both his arms. It started to twist and roll. For every two spins the beast made, Jorge only made one.

Everyone screamed. Pete ran down the bank and grabbed the monster by the head, trying to pry its mouth open. I ran and jumped on its back to stop the death roll. I felt claws tear into my side. Jorge's arms could be heard breaking above his screams. Sand filled my eyes. Pete and I were able to stop the alligator from spinning, but it wouldn't release its grip.

Marcos began stabbing at it with his atlatl, but the small wooden shaft was no match for the tough natural armor.

"Its eyes!" I yelled.

He jabbed at the eyes several times missing every attempt. Finally one poke hit its mark as did the next three, and the reptile let go. It turned, throwing both Pete and me on the sand. As it entered the water Pete landed one punch, then it was gone.

Jorge lay unconscious.

Maria was on him before anyone. "Get me something for bandages. Quick!"

I could see his arms were disjointed but didn't seem to be bleeding as bad as I thought they would be. I sat down to rest. My heart pounded hard enough to cause pain. Wrestling an alligator required far more physical effort than one could imagine. Catching my breath seemed nearly impossible. The longer I sat, the more the pain increased. I didn't tell Beth because she was busy with Jorge. Trying to stand, I stumbled. Weakness overcame me. I lay down and fell asleep.

"Wake up. Get away from this river," Beth said. As she helped me up she asked, "Are you okay?"

I was still experiencing chest pain, but wouldn't tell her. "Yeah. How's he doing?"

"Both shoulders are dislocated, and his radius and ulna are broken in each arm. They were compound fractures. We stopped the bleeding, but I'm worried about infection. We splinted him up, but I don't know how much damage is done inside."

My pains remained. I couldn't help but think about my insides too.

In the week following the attack Jorge used up many of the painkillers. His arms were both mangled and hung down at his side uselessly. Tendons and ligaments had been torn. In the past, doctors could have repaired the damage. The girls did all they could just to save his life.

The first time the sun appeared, the nurses looked at his wounds. In this different light the true colors came out. Both arms were starting to show signs of gangrene.

"We're going to have to amputate both your arms below the shoulder, Jorge." Maria told him. "We can help with painkillers, but I'm not sure we can knock you out."

"Why don't you give me a few more and leave me behind? I'm not going to be any help to the rest of you. I'm not even going to be able to help you with Emanuel."

"That's not going to happen," Beth said. "You can still watch the kids. The rest of us can help out with the chores."

"I won't even be able to feed myself. I won't even be able to hug Emanuel!" Jorge started crying. "I can't even cover my face!" His right arm flailed not quite reaching his neck, the bandaged hand dangling uncontrollably. His left arm moved no more.

Maria hugged him and shielded his face from the rest of while he sobbed.

Sarah motioned to Beth and me to follow her away from the two. As we walked she spoke in a low tone. "We can take both at the same time, but I can't guarantee he will live, or for how long after."

"Can't you take one now, and then the other after he recovers from the first?" I asked. "I would think he might bleed to death doing two amputations at the same time."

"We can control the bleeding safely enough," Sarah said, "but he's already feverish and the infection will kill him if we don't do something now."

"Have you ever done one?" Beth asked Sarah. "I never have. In these conditions I think we might kill him."

"No, but he'll die if we don't. I studied about Civil War amputations in the field. There were cases about people who amputated their own arms. It can be done. I think we make sure he eats and hydrates himself well before we do it. He should be okay for another couple more days."

"What will you need from me? Pete and I will start looking for canned food again."

"Look for paper clips too. We can use them for clamps. Also get any cloth you can. We're going to need a lot of it." Sarah looked at Beth. "Can you think of any other way?"

Beth stood thinking a while then said with a shaky voice, "We're going to need a saw."

I got up early to build a good bed of coals. Several pots of water needed to be brought to a rolling boil for instrument sterilization. Cloth needed to be washed and then dried for bandages.

My plan was to have it all done before anyone got up, but I tired easily and needed to rest more than usual. Pains accompanied the breathlessness. Today's work was too important to be stopped by a little chest pain.

Beth's morning round of vomiting woke Jorge, who I'm sure didn't sleep much anyway.

"Getting everything ready, huh?" He sat next to me as his arms dangled.

"Wanna make sure we do this quick," I said.

"I'm scared, Nick. I don't think I can take it. I'm not as tough as you and Pete."

"You'll do fine. You do know Pete said he's going to change your nickname from George to Stumpy. Just thought you should know." I looked at him to see his reaction.

He looked at both of his arms and said, "You know I used to throw coal at him and try to hit him on the helmet. I missed most of the time, but even when I hit him right in the face, he never got mad. He'd just say, 'Is that the best you can do?' then go right back to work. He's a good friend." His smile appeared. "I would love to be able to throw something at him now."

Sarah dropped four knives into the boiling water. She looked into the other pots to see their progress. "This one needs to be hotter." She inspected the cloth on the drying rack. "These need to be drier." Then she walked over to Beth and helped her recover from her morning's purging.

When the cloth was dry and the water boiled, all three nurses came over to Jorge and said it was time. They gave him five eighty-milligram Oxycotins. And explained what he would experience once they started. He listened bravely but trembled violently.

Marcos kept the children away from the arena.

A bed of beaver pelts served as the operating table. Torches surrounded the area. A boiling pot of water held the butcher knives and paper clips.

Jorge lay down shirtless on the furs.

Pete knelt down next to him. "Don't get a hard on George, or I will jump off! So help me God!" With that said, he straddled his friend. Then he got serious. "I want you to know Gorge: I'm only doing this for you. I have been to hell and back with you more than once. I'm at *your* side this time. Now get tough little buddy! I love you." He gritted his teeth.

Jorge gritted his back, but it still looked like a forced smile.

Pete reached down to hold his arms.

Jorge closed his eyes.

Beth placed her hand on the inside of Jorge's inner arm to apply pressure to his artery.

"Take a big breath. This will be done before you know it." Sarah began to cut a circle in his right elbow.

Jorge's whole body convulsed as he screamed. Pete threw his whole weight on his friend's arms, pinning him to the bed.

Maria kissed and caressed his head while she cried. "You're doing this for Emanuel and me. Remember he needs you. I love you, I love you. Jesus, watch over my husband for the sake of his child. Take away his pain and lessen his fever. Help Sarah and Beth..."

Jorge's screams were replaced by moaning. He passed out from the pain.

Beth said nothing. Her fingers tightened on her patient's pressure point.

Sarah peeled skin back and held it there with paper clips. Muscle was cut to reveal white tendons and ligaments. Muscle was cut from the bone but left in place. With three inches of bone showing above the elbow Sarah picked up the hacksaw.

Both Pete and I held his arm as she sawed. Beth controlled the bleeding while Maria wept.

Chapter 41
New Duties for Jorge

Maria and Sarah laid down their arm full of roots, enough for one meal.

"I don't know how you did this day after day. My hands are more wrinkled than if I had been doing dishes for a month." Sarah showed her hands to Jorge. "Have the kids been any trouble?"

"No." The children minded Jorge without being scolded. Somehow they knew when he spoke they were to behave. "Maria I have to pee." He'd healed well from the operation, but his spirit was damaged still.

The two of them walked off away from view and earshot.

"Stupid ass! Here I go showing an armless man my wrinkled hands," Sarah said hitting herself in the head as punishment.

Pete whispered to me, "We've got to find him something else to do besides babysitting. A man needs to feel useful. I could build some sort of cart he could tow to carry supplies. He could hook it to his shoulders."

"Can you build one?" My body needed a break. Both Beth and I had needed to take more rest stops in the last few months.

"I'll look around for bike parts." Pete was the engineer of the group.

"Where's Marcos?" I asked.

"He's down at the culvert setting his crayfish trap. He said he was going to wait there for something to come out. Do you want me to go check on him?"

"No," I said. "He knows what he's doing. Let him hunt."

Maria and Jorge returned.

Beth motioned to the nurses. "Can I talk to you?" Most of their private talks concerned her pregnancy. She had started to show. They huddled together. Both Sarah and Maria were ever observant of Beth's progress. She was to stay at camp and lie still and was no longer expected to be involved in any chores whatsoever. They estimated her weight to be at a dangerously low level and worried about the baby.

I was worried about both. I felt tremendous guilt that I hadn't been able to provide enough for everyone, but most of all for her. Now my unborn child was in jeopardy. This was the first time I felt a real sense of impending doom. It was either that or a symptom of my chest pains, which never really seemed to go totally away.

"Look what I got." Marcos strode into sight and held up an opossum and a can. "I got about fifty snails too." Marcos loved to gather them. It took hundreds of them to make a difference, but Marcos felt good doing his part. I was his best customer. How could I resist them? When others were dining on roots, I was eating escargot, shells and all. Nobody else would eat them.

He held up his big catch. "I found its den and waited and waited. Then I heard a scratching sound. I got ready, and when I saw its head, I waited some more, till I saw the whole body. Then I stabbed it in the chest. Man, it tried to bite me and hissed and growled." He shook the rat looking thing in the air and smiled wide.

Weeks went by until Pete found everything he needed to construct the cart—a cross between a rickshaw and a cart used in harness racing. Eventually plans evolved into a finished product. Seatbelts tucked away underneath seats of rusting cars were salvaged for adjustable harnesses. When it was introduced to Jorge, his smile came back for the first time since his operation.

"Load it up, I can carry it." He bounced up and down adjusting the harness. "Make a spot for Manny too. It's not heavy at all."

"Beth can hold him." Sarah started taking things off the cart. "She'll be riding back here until she has the baby."

"Doesn't matter to me, as long as I'm doing something. I can carry you all," Jorge boasted.

Selfishly, I hated the idea of carrying my share. I grew winded easily and would need frequent rests, but now I wouldn't be able to blame it on Beth.

Nobody argued, and we moved on, looking in every cellar that we came upon. We were back to eating from cans again, or at least Beth was. She needed different vitamins, and fats that we weren't getting from the wild game. Sarah had been adamant about extra rations being given to Beth.

"Give the beans to Beth this time Nick, she needs the fat." Apparently Beth had told Sarah about the beans. I didn't even think she knew.

Our diet consisted of fifty percent canned foods and fifty percent wild game. Muskrats which had been so plentiful in the past seemed uncatchable. Beavers didn't seem to exist in this area. Few large animals were being caught lately.

One day while Maria was feeding Manny, Jorge started jumping around like he was on fire.

"Stop it! I'm going to fall off," Beth yelled. "What to hell are you doing?"

From the light of the torch I watched him jumping up and down from one foot to another.

I could see a snake slither under Jorge's feet. At first I thought he was just trying to get away from it, but he followed it as it came closer to the children. He spun the cart around, a hundred and eighty degrees, nearly knocking Beth off. The snake lunged at his legs, but his foot caught it short and Jorge finished it off with his other foot. Bones crunched below the workboot's sole. Even after the head had been crushed, the tail still vibrated.

"There. Now we have something to eat tonight. Marcos, come see what I got. Look, it has a rattle too. That would make a great addition to your necklace." His smile was back.

"The next time you decide to River Dance, let me know first, okay?" Beth seemed unimpressed. "Fuck the snake! Help me up on this friggin' thing."

I shifted her weight up towards Jorge. "Is that too heavy?"

He jumped to adjust the straps shaking his head in the negative. No teeth showing.

Beth extended one leg, and then put both knees up to her stomach. A few seconds later she would straighten the other leg, and raise both arms over her head. She rolled my way and sternly said, "Just walk with me and hold my hand...Please."

We walked like that for the remaining months of her pregnancy.

Jorge let me say, "Giddy up," but only once.

Chapter 42
Building Jorge's Confidence

Marcos, the newly designated scout, ran faster, farther and longer than anyone else in the group. He marked the road with stones for us to follow. When he found a good place to camp, he'd gather wood and look for food. The rest of us would catch up. Sometimes he'd have food, most times not. Occasionally cans of food or headless turtles were left in the middle of the road instead of stone markers.

"As much as I hate riding on this thing, I do like the idea of holding your hand while we walk. Do you know we haven't held hands since before we were married? Why did we stop?"

"I don't know," I said. "Just kind of grew out of it I guess."

"You did. I didn't." Beth squeezed harder on my hand. "You know I really love you."

"I love you too, babe."

"Do you know what I love most about you?" she asked.

"My good looks?" To tell the truth, I hadn't looked at myself in a mirror since this started. I wasn't even sure what I looked like anymore. I rubbed my beard and tried to imagine.

"Not even close," she joked. "I've always felt safe with you. Even when everything shit to bed, you saved me. You saved me the day I met you. You changed my life. Now I'm having your baby. I couldn't be prouder to be your wife. I want to have a family again, Nick. I miss my babies." She started to cry. "I don't want to lose this one too. I can't take another loss." She continued to sob.

Sarah brought Tara and Eve up to walk along Beth's other side.

Beth let go of my hand to hold Tara's.

"Mommy, ride?" Tara asked.

"No, you can walk. You're a big girl now." She held her hand on Tara's head.

"Everything's going to be fine. Sarah and Maria won't let anything happen." Trying to change the subject I asked, "Do you think I can be a good dad?"

"I know you will." She sniffed and wiped her eyes. "Just watch Jorge. He's a great dad."

"Thank you." Smiling as he turned, Jorge's inattention caused a wheel to run over one of Marco's stone markers.

Beth yelled out in pain. The cart had no shock absorbers. "You just keep walking straight up there, and try not to hit all the bumps please."

"I didn't do much with your kids. I was always afraid to cross boundaries. I felt they didn't respect me and kept my distance. I'm scared about raising this one."

"You'll do fine. Marcos loves you. He shadows you like a dog."

"I don't know what I did to cause that. I always felt Marcos didn't like me because I was always telling him what to do."

"You were teaching him, hon, that's what dads do."

"I'm not his dad. Never wanted to be."

"It'll be ok." She held her stomach. "I'll help you."

Jorge stopped in mid stride. "You're going to have to get off." He slipped out from underneath the straps leaving me holding Beth. She hadn't time to dismount.

"What are you doing?" She asked as her feet hit the pavement.

Jorge ran up the road. We missed what he obviously saw from a distance. Once again he stomped on something with a killing force. "Got another one," he yelled.

Pete and I walked up to see what he found. Another snake, but this one didn't have a rattle.

The peculiar thing was that the serpent had been held down by two flat rocks. One blow from either stone could have killed it, but it was left there for Jorge, alive and easily found.

"Looks like we're on the right path." Pete laughed. "Maybe Marcos will have a fire started so we can cook George's trophy.

Beth climbed back on, I hitched Jorge up and we were on our way again.

Chapter 43
Splitting Up

"Nick, we've got to find her some place dry and clean for her to have this baby." According to Sarah's calculations Beth was in her eighth month. "I'm not going to let her drop this kid beside the road."

Our goal to find shelter and food to last a month or two seemed unreachable. Long distances between towns or houses, not to mention rivers or swamps made travelling long distances imperative. Sitting out the rain and only moving during dry days would cause our supplies to run out. We were eating food as fast as we found it.

"We're wasting time going down roads leading us nowhere," Sarah said. "Send the guys up ahead to find shelter."

"I can't do it. I have to stay with Beth." In reality I couldn't walk far without sitting down to take a break. I would lose my wind within the first half mile, and I couldn't take Jorge's place pulling Beth, I just didn't have it in me.

Marcos took off in one direction, Pete in another. The rest of us huddled under the beaver-skin tarp for one of them to return. Rain was an obstacle the scouts had to ignore.

While waiting, Beth's water broke.

About halfway through the day, Pete came running back. "I found a granary. The building is still standing, and there should be plenty of rats and grain. I didn't check it out or build a fire. As soon as I saw it I came back to get you." He struggled to catch his breath.

"We can't wait any longer. Take us to it," Sarah ordered.

"We can't leave Marcos behind," I said as I threw pots and pans next to Beth on the gurney. "Pete did you mark the way?"

"Some of the way, but I forgot in a few places. But I can recognize it when I see it," Pete said, ruling him out as the one who would stay and wait for Marcos.

I looked around. "Maria, do you mind waiting for him? He shouldn't be too long.

Sarah never gave Maria time to speak. "No, Nick. I'm going to need her. You wait for him. There's nothing you can do now. Wait here and get some sleep. You're going to need it.

Maria spoke up. "Let's not forget about Manny. And what if Jorge has to pee? Do you want to help him Nick?"

"Jorge, drive slow. You're carrying my family with you. Watch out for traffic." I smiled at Beth.

"I shouldn't be far behind you. Wait for me if you can."

All three nurses laughed in reflex.

"Yes, dear. I'll hold it in until you get there. Give me a kiss. I'm sure you have a few hours."

We kissed. "You wait for me, okay?" I patted her tummy and gave her another kiss.

The torchlight dimmed and darkness accompanied a feeling of complete isolation. The thought of following Marcos vanished after the first quarter mile, so I sat down and decided to wait for his return. I immediately started worrying about Beth. I knew she was in good hands, but still wanted to be there.

I also didn't want to risk losing Marcos. Although he has been out on his own for months now, I didn't want to take that chance.

Listening to the sounds around me, I noticed nothing but insects making a noise so loud one would think he were standing next to high tension electrical equipment, a constant buzz combined with several different octaves of humming. Chirps, clicks and whistles broke the monotony in no recognizable pattern. The drone of wings filled the sky, unseen, but still felt, as much as heard.

Memories flashed of a world long gone. Imagining how life was before was like trying to remember a dream hours after waking up. Each time I thought about people from the days of sunshine,

I would forget what they looked like as soon as I opened my eyes. Their features would disappear in the darkness. The memories since were difficult to erase. Mick's face, the children's blood in the snow, Beth and the preacher, all burned in my mind as I tried to sleep. I lay in the middle of the road so Marcos wouldn't walk by me. The rains had washed the soot and ash off long ago, but the road was hard as ever. I couldn't lie flat on my back. I couldn't breathe. I tried to lie on my side, but my arm would fall asleep. I would doze off, then wake up, fall asleep again, only to toss and turn.

Bright light blinded me through closed eyelids. I held up my hand to block the sun, first time in weeks. I looked around at my surroundings. No sign of life for miles. Then down the road, I saw smoke in the distance. It was Marcos. He was on his way back. The black smoke of his torch left a trail lingering in the air as he ran. The ribbons of carbon disappeared, to be replaced by a dim long lazy flame. The sun vanished under cloud again, making his the only light left.

Chapter 44
Labor Day

"Where is everybody?" Marcos asked.

"Beth's having the baby. They all went to a shelter with Pete. Come on. We have to get going. I need to be with Beth."

"But I found some great signs. I know I could catch something if I go back."

"Marcos, I can't leave you. Pete says there should be food where they are."

"But Nick, I know where possums are holed up. I found tons of poop. I'm not a little boy anymore you know."

I looked at him and smiled. Patting him on the shoulder, I said, "No, you've grown up a lot lately." I realized that I was a big part of that, and smiled wider. "Okay, but don't be too long, and be careful. Do you think you could find your way back to the rest of us if I mark the road?" I didn't want to leave him, but Beth needed me.

"I'll be fine. Tell Beth I'll be praying for her."

I turned around. "Where did you learn that?"

"Maria taught me a few prayers and said if I prayed more, I would catch more animals. I tried

it and it works. I guess it might work for the baby...
kinda."

"I'll tell her." I left him and hurried along,
checking every intersection for signs of the others,
adding to the rocks shaped like an arrow marking
our direction. There was no chance of Marcos getting lost. I would stop at every culvert to inspect
for sign, and to catch my breath. If I found good
sign, I'd mark it for him. He had more time to look
it over and set traps if he thought it was promising.

Less than a mile after the last marker, the
silhouette of a tower could be made out from the
dim light released by the clouds. At first glimpse, I
knew it wasn't what Pete thought it was. Still I hurried uphill to get to Beth, listening for the sound
of a newborn's cry between each labored breath,
(mine, not Beth's). The pains were back, but only
another hundred yards remained till I was back
with my wife. I pushed myself.

Pete met me at the entrance.

"How's she doing?" I asked as I held my chest.

"She still hasn't had it. Come on, I'll bring
you to her. I'm sorry, Nick. I thought it was a place
that made grain. It's just a cement plant."

"At least she has a dry place to have it." I was
disappointed about the lack of food.

Pete led me into a room covered with dust.
Beth was lying on a bed of beaver skins in the middle of the room. Two torches lit the area.

I leaned over Beth. "How you doing, babe?

She licked her dry lips. "I'm hungry." A contraction caused her back to convulse as pain coursed through her body.

After the contraction subsided, she again asked for something to eat, but this time she addressed Sarah. "Nurse, can you get me some Jell-O, or sherbet?" The sweat was pooling on her brow, then the surface tension reached its maximum and some dripped down the side of her face.

Sarah smiled at Beth. "No... all I can let you have is some ice chips." They both had said the same thing a thousand times before.

"Do we have anything to eat?" This time she was looking at me.

I didn't want to tell her that in fact we had nothing. "Sarah told you, you can't have anything. I'll get you some water. No ice."

"Wait," Beth grabbed my arm. "Where's Marcos?"

"Marcos is okay and on his way here, but he wanted to stop and look for food. He'll be fine."

"Oh, I know he will. You taught him well," Beth said forcing a smile.

"He said he would pray for you." I watched her face for some reaction, but got none. "I'll get your water."

When I returned with the water, Beth was talking to Maria, and both of them were crying.

"What's wrong?" I asked.

Holding Maria's hand, Beth said, "I just told Maria that if anything should happen to me she could raise Tara and the baby as Christians."

"Nothing's going to happen. Stop talking stupid," I told her.

"I want them to believe that there is a reason to go on. All you have to do is believe, and be good, and you go to heaven. As long as you believe and try your best, you are at peace."

"I thought you didn't believe in heaven?"

"Nick, you know I don't believe in God because of my science. I didn't talk to God when I was in that tunnel because I know he doesn't exist. In my opinion, religions seem to be based on legends, and cannot be proven by any evidence, so that's why…"

Maria let go of Beth's hand, stepped back and crossed her arms.

Beth stopped briefly, losing her train of thought. "It doesn't matter. Science has suffered a sizeable setback. It will be centuries before man can get back to where he was before this happened. With the future the kids will have, they will need faith.

Maria could hold her tongue no longer. "Beth, you think you know a lot about science, right?" She held Beth's hand again.

"Yea, probably more than most. I was a teacher," Beth answered.

"Well ... " Maria hesitated. "When I was studying to be an X-ray tech, for two, three days they taught about the atom, and all the things it was made of. They talked about Einstein, parallel universes, eleven dimensions and particles that they haven't even seen yet. It was all over my head, and I knew I would never see it again. But what if..." She paused again. "What if, one of those extra dimensions, is where God lives? What if one of those particles they haven't even seen yet, is proof of God? Maybe we're part of God, or he's part of us. Maybe we're both connected in a quantum dimension that science didn't have time to discover."

Beth was silent.

Maria continued, "Isn't it possible that God does exist and you haven't found him yet? Isn't there still a chance you could open your mind to God?"

All three of us stood aghast looking at Maria. She had seldom spoken, let alone spoken out.

Beth stuck to her guns. "Unfortunately, I know what will happen to me if I die giving birth. My knowledge of science leads me to believe that when I die, my consciousness will become nonexistent. I will have no knowledge of ever being. My body will rot and ... "

"Now that's enough." She was quitting already, and I wasn't going to put up with it. "You're talking stupid. You've got two experienced nurses who both have helped deliver babies before. You're going to be fine. Now talk about something happier... Please."

She rubbed my arm. "I think it's going to be a long delivery, hon. You better get some sleep while you can."

I slept beside Beth and was only awoken occasionally by her moaning.

Chapter 45
Praying

I was startled by Beth's scream. "What's wrong?" I asked Sarah. "How long have I been asleep?"

Beth grabbed my hand and squeezed.

"Are you okay?" My hand went numb.

Sarah took me aside. "Beth's having a dry birth, Nick. This is going to be hard on her. You really need to be by her side. She's been in hard labor for hours now. We've got to get this kid out of her."

"What I can I do?"

Sarah asked, "Are you an atheist like she is? If not, then praying would be my suggestion."

Her contractions spanned only about two minutes apart for what seemed like hours.

"Maria, are those towels dry yet?" Sarah asked. Beth had already soaked the ones under her with blood.

"Nick you better stay by her side from now on," Sarah said.

"What's wrong?" I asked.

Beth latched onto my hand. "I'm hemorrhaging, babe. I've been at this too long and my old body isn't up to it. You're going to have raise this baby by yourself, sweetheart. I think that once I'm done with this I won't have much more left."

With a shaky voice I tried to scold her. "You just think positive and don't you dare give up. Damn it! You know I won't be any good at raising a kid. I need you. Now you just stop thinking stupid thoughts and try to relax and let that kid slip out."

She tried to laugh, and her fake smile reminded me of the good times before this nightmare.

Instantly I was transported to a time of camping amongst the forest, when they held lush green leaves, not just scorched trunks, void of branches.

I remembered our grandbabies' faces when Ninny bought them a new swing that Papa had to put together.

I had thousands of memories about hunting trips I had taken, but the times when she accompanied me were the most memorable.

I remembered all the fun the two of us had at the fundraisers for the fire department. I was so proud to be seen with her. Her beautiful red hair draped over my arm as we danced. Of course my other hand was on her cute little ass. Everyone who watched us was envious of our love and lust.

In fact, she was in every good time that I could remember.

"Okay, finally. We've got crowning... That a girl. Push ... Push...Push..." Sarah said.

In between breaths, Beth yelled, "I am... Whew, Whew, Whew!" she continued her metronomic breathing.

I knew Beth was giving it everything she had. She said she had one more job to do, and I was watching her do it.

"Come on, honey, just a little more." I looked at Sarah. The same fear I felt, was clear on her face.

"Maria, bring some more towels, and pack her tightly please." Sarah was holding our child's head in her in her hands. A few seconds later she said, "It's a boy." She immediately handed our son to Maria and turned her attentions to Beth.

Beth and I were crying in unison as violently as possible, without making a sound.

Once she caught her breath she ordered, "Name him Phoenix." She gasped for more air. "I want you to concentrate on teaching Marcos... all the survival skills you know...he will be the one who teaches the young ones. Once the elders pass on... he will teach your son. It's your duty to teach him... so he can teach Phoenix."

"Just hold on and you can help me. You will be fine after you rest." I choked for more words.

"Shh... Maria has enough milk for both Phoenix and Emanuel... Sarah and Pete said they will take Tara." She trembled, but continued to speak. "Maria and Jorge will help out with the baby." Her breathing increased, but speaking was more important than air. Tell Marcos..." She took three short breaths, and then slipped away without kissing me goodbye. My emotional mucus plug had come out, and like Beth, I bled out there that night.

I felt a sudden horrible emptiness come over me for the first time in my life. Sarah handed me my new son. I looked at him, scarcely able to make out his thin, but obviously red hair in the dim light.

I kissed her, then him, as I wept.

Maria said prayers for her soul, and then slipped the necklace with the cross on Beth's neck.

Chapter 46
Alone

All I could do was sit there and watch as Pete dug her grave. A sand pile behind the steel building would be Beth's final resting place, for no other reason other than easy digging. Pete's body had emaciated to the point his muscles ached. He struggled, but still found the strength to help Maria and Sarah lower Beth into the shallow grave. Her body, wrapped in a cocoon of beaver skins, soon disappeared under a pile of sand meant to bond cement to make concrete.

"No! We can't leave her here. Something will dig her up. It's not deep enough." I ran to the pile and started pulling sand off the mound.

Pete grabbed me, "Nick, I found some sidewalk tiles on the other side of the building. We are going to place them over her grave as a marker. They will keep anything out."

I knelt in the sand thinking. "Okay, but I want to place them. You guys take a break. This is something I want to do alone."

Pete helped me carry them all over to the sand pile, and then joined the others.

My main concern was to keep animals away from her body. As I placed the tiles on sand, I interlocked each one as tightly as possible, lifting each one several times. My fingers bled from jamming them between pieces. My back hurt and pain radiated down my legs, but I continued. This act of covering her body to prevent scavengers wasn't enough. How could I mark her grave so others would know who she was? Maybe letting Maria put the cross on her neck was a bad idea. But it wouldn't matter to Beth now. I didn't have the energy to get fancy. I just wanted to finish. I had to stop and catch my breath.

"You okay over there? Take your time," Sarah said.

"Almost done." I forced myself back to work. My chest pains had come back about the time Phoenix was crowning. I'd learned to ignore them, but these were the worst. A half dozen blocks remained and I wouldn't quit until it was finished. I dropped with five left.

"Hey, you ok?" Sarah said running to my aid.

"Yeah, I just need a longer break." I couldn't catch my breath, but tried to get back up.

She held my wrist as she guided me to the ground. "Sit down and we will finish that. Now slow down your breathing and relax."

"No, I want to make sure it's right." My left arm went numb, and both hands tingled. "I have to finish this now." My breathing escalated. I tried to stand.

"You've got to slow your breathing down. You're hyperventilating."

"She deserves...better...than this." I tried to yell, but didn't have the wind.

Sarah held my chin with one hand. "Nick, you have to calm down!

I needed more air, and pushed her hand away. I needed to breathe, but her hand was obstructing me. I thrashed trying to push her away.

She firmly held my head in both hands. "Nick, calm down and listen to me. I'm going to help you breathe. I'm going to place my mouth on yours and we are going to breath into each other's lungs. Do you understand? Trust me." She then lowered her mouth to meet mine.

I tried to fight her, but couldn't.

Her breath was hot, but I couldn't get enough of it. I sucked for more. She held the seal so tight, controlling my intake, no fresh air got through. After three rounds of controlled breathing, my fight evaporated. I accepted what she was doing. Her lungs took the place of a brown bag. After about a minute she pulled away.

"There now keep taking slow deep breaths. Slow...That's good."

"I want to be buried alongside her." I took another measured inhalation.

"You're not going to die today. You're just having a panic attack. You've been through a lot lately. Do you have any pains in your neck or arm?"

"No, but my chest feels like someone is standing on it. I feel like I am dying. I feel so bad that I haven't done enough to keep everyone from starving to death. If Beth had been fed better, she would probably still be alive." My breathing increased.

"Slow down. Slow down your breathing and be quiet a minute, I want to listen to your heart." Sarah lowered her head, placing her ear on my chest. "Everyone quiet!" Everyone obeyed, except for the insects. She kept moving her head to different areas of my chest. Then she moved to my back.

Sarah backed away and knelt on the sand. "First of all let me say this: Beth might have survived if she had more food, maybe she was just too old. She did have enough energy to give you a son. Phoenix is going to need you. Marcos still needs you. You still have a job to do." She held my hand. "You will get the time to do it." She put her other hand on my leg. "But you have to take it easy. That means you get to ride Jorge from now on." The woman, who just open mouth kissed me for two minutes, looked at me with a wink of reassurance.

As doomed as I thought I was, I looked at Jorge, his big stupid grin looking me right in the face. I burst out laughing, tears running down my face. Everyone joined in, hugging and kissing me when I needed it most. Again I felt drained emotionally, but I needed it. We were family, and I felt loved.

Pete grabbed a stone, so did Sarah and Maria. The children tried to lift them. I watched while I rested. I knew one of them would pinch a finger, but I let it go on. The last of the blocks were placed, securing Beth's resting place.

The sun poked out from behind thick clouds. Her grave looked very nice and secure, nothing more than she would have wanted. Maria wanted to place a cross to mark it. I said no.

I saw a shadow move along the road in the distance. It was Marcos running, dangling an opossum by the tail in each hand. He found us.

To my left, one of the babies dropped a stone on her fingers while piling stones up like the big people did. The rest came to her rescue.

I left them alone, except to say, "Sometimes we need to learn things the hard way." Then I lay down to take a much-needed nap.

Epilogue
The Cyclical Earth

The rogue moon that slammed into the Earth at 60,000 miles per hour was formed 6.5 billion years ago in another solar system in the Milky Way galaxy. As two giant gas planets collided, the little moon was ejected out into space, never to orbit its star again. Though small as moons go, the thirty-seven-mile rock travelled in a straight line while our solar system and home planet were still being formed. Approaching from behind our sun, after traveling for billions of years, it remained undetected until a day and a half from impact.

Impact: When the tiny moon slammed the planet's crust, ejecta circled the world, lighting fires and baking everything above ground for two days. Nineteen percent of all species went extinct immediately. Others followed as the process of photosynthesis stopped, and the food chain fell apart.

1 month AI (After Impact): Four thousand, three hundred twelve people survived the first month of the disaster.

3.5 years AI: When supplies ran out at underground bunkers, those who counted on them soon starved to death. Mankind had forgotten to teach the basic skills of survival that had sustained them a couple thousand years earlier. They relied on their technologies, infrastructures, and governments. Few had the ability to provide for themselves under the conditions that existed.

51 years AI: The eruption of the super volcano located beneath Yellowstone national park would signal the end of the Anthropocene epoch: a period of geological time that began with the industrial revolution, when man began to affect the planet with his pollutants on a grand scale. This was the final blow for any homo sapiens that had survived the impact. Arrogantly, they thought that they would be the most advanced living beings that ever inhabited the planet Earth. They imagined themselves eventually spreading out into the universe to encounter other worlds and other species. Colonizing Mars never happened, leaving man a one planet species: a disadvantage in a violent universe.

52 years AI: Humans go extinct like 99.99 percent of all species that ever lived on the planet. Mass extinctions are not uncommon, there have been at least five major events before this one in the past.

The Second Intelligent Species

The only land containing life larger than an insect was the North and South American continents. Europe and Africa were no longer recognizable; layers of molten rock covered one half of the globe. Other than the coastline, the western hemisphere geographically, had not been changed.

After the dust settled, the balance returned. Life continued, just as it had sixty-five million years before. Several small ice ages left only the equatorial areas able to prosper for an extended period of time. Only the tropics escaped the snow.

The sun was permitted to reach the ground again and its energy was welcomed by the living that remained. The Earth was new again. The slate had been wiped clean again.

Ferns were plentiful. Insects devoured them as fast as they would grow; they thrived, feeding on the dead, the new growth, and each other. Animals that fed on insects adapted and soon became the most successful species of the new period.

Mice, moles, rats, bats and shrews made up most of the mammal life that remained on the two continents. Common house cats survived and hunted once again.

Opossums were the last of the marsupials.

Reptiles seemed unharmed, and were plentiful.

The amphibians that didn't go extinct during the time of man came out of the mud and continued on, though there were few.

Birds didn't make it this time; the dinosaurs finally went extinct.

During the day, insects would feed on the ground, clearing any vegetation that would grow. Plant growth never had the chance to come back to where it had been.

At night opossums and bats gorged on the insects.

The reptiles would eat anything that passed by.

Time went on for the earth as it always did. Man was not missed.

Fifty-five million years slowly passed: a mere hiccup in Earth's life.

The oceans were alive again and the climate leveled off to a more temperate one.

Plant life adapted to change in their new world. Their leaves became tough and toxic to prevent total loss from predation. Even those plants whose entirety remained under ground could not escape the hordes of insects.

Mammals advanced, but competed with the swarms of insects that darkened the skies during the day, and never amounted to anything larger than an average sized rodent.

Reptiles survived just the way that they had all the other times that the earth had gone through this cleansing process. They didn't evolve into much more than they already were. They had already developed a successful design, though they did get smaller.

The opossums gave up their nocturnal habits. Food was easier to find in the sunlight, plus using their prehensile tails to see over the ever present ferns, they could keep an eye out for their only predator: feral cats. Eventually, they learned to walk upright, though it was more like skipping, and resembled the way the astronauts of Apollo 11 walked on the moon. Opossums had a jump on all other species when it came to evolution. They already had something like an opposable thumb and were quick to learn how use it. They had a remarkable immune system; they were less likely to succumb to snakebite than the mammals. They retained their acute sense of smell and their tails. Eventually they began to eat only insects and small mammals, they became strictly carnivores. Their brains grew because of their new high protein diet.

Marsupaloids began to hunt in groups and in time they started farming insects, and rodents. The earth was home to its second intelligent species. Eventually they developed a form of communication. A combination of scents, body language and tail gestures utilizing a form of mathematics more complicated than most humans were aware even existed. During the fourth ice age since the impact, they migrated across what was the Bering Strait, taking the same path that some early men had once taken, but going in the opposite direction. They learned to use some of the tools they had found from the time of the humans, and eventually, why homo sapiens went extinct. From the evidence found, it was believed their extinction was caused by an impact.

The fossil evidence was discovered just as it was in the time of man. Specialists in the field of paleontology and geology worked the areas where evidence of man's past could still be found.

On a hot day, in what was the mid-eastern North American continent, an assistant to the head of paleontology slowly took the diamond artifact from the mummified remains of one of the last humans and slipped it into her pouch. Undiscovered, she continued her work. She then took the necklace from around the neck of the fossil; behind one of the vertebra laid a cross, similar to the hundreds of thousands of others found in the lower half of the continent. They knew this symbol was important to the humans, but still needed to learn more.

The Marsupaloids copied the technology of man and soon learned to harvest the same fossil fuels the humans did to power their earlier machines.

'It's not the strongest of the species that survives, nor the most intelligent that survives. It is the one that is the most adaptable to change.' Charles Darwin

THE END

Made in the USA
Charleston, SC
11 March 2013